2020

The Year

400

Bill de Garis

Cover scene: The Pacific Northwest of North America

This is the fourth novel of the 2020 series
Book 1: **2020 After the End**
Book 2: **2020 The Long Walk**
Book 3: **2020 Africa**

Contents

Prologue

2020—Part 4, The Year 400

Prologue (What happened in books 1, 2 and 3).

There's no need to read this prologue if you have read all the previous books. Just go straight to chapter one. Although there is some new stuff towards the end.

In book 1 "2020 After the End", PJ, Kacie, Mike, and Jeff travelled south to Baja, Mexico, as they tried to escape a coming ice-age winter in BC, Canada. A meteor had triggered not only giant waves and earthquakes all over the world but also a nuclear war. The combined effect was the collapse of civilisation and the lengthening of the year to two and a half times longer than it was before. It was a real mess. Death and destruction seemed absolute to those still alive. No one who survived could quite believe what had happened. The greatest threat to our survival was the lengthening of the seasons. The meteor's size and gravitational tug on the earth changed the earth's tilt and precession and even altered its orbit around the sun. So with the knowledge that the seasons were ten months instead of four the friends knew they had to go south if they wanted to live. They knew they wouldn't survive the cold of the northern winter.

They had to fight their way past the dregs of humanity seeking to rob and pillage them. On the way they met up with several other people, old friends and new, who joined them. Among them was Dale the redneck farmer from Walla Walla near the border with Oregon, and the Boneman from Mount Shasta in northern California.

They all eventually make it to safety in Baja where the pleasant temperatures enabled them to grow food in the winter. They survived stuff they never thought possible: big things like violent attacks, and everyday things like having no heat or electricity. They learned to find water and purify it, to chop wood for heat or to make shelters, to hunt for food, and to grow food from seeds. It was pretty amazing because they all came from multiple generations that had had life way too easy… tv's, phones, computers, hot and cold water from the tap, food in the grocery store, delivery, takeout, and of course entertainment anytime they wanted it. This group proved they were tough enough to live through what the majority of civilization, after generations of being civilized, could not. The winter they survived was a frozen wasteland in North America, all the way from the Arctic through to northern California on the west and Mississippi and Georgia on the east. In the centre it was frozen all the way down to central and parts of southern Arizona and New Mexico, and well south of the Texas Panhandle. There was five feet of snow in Amarillo that didn't go away until the start of summer this year. Like the wildebeest in the Serengeti of East Africa, the few humans left have to migrate every year to stay alive. And just like the wildebeest having to cross the Mara river and falling prey to giant crocodiles, so too do our friends have serious dangers to overcome.

In book 2 "2020 The Long Walk" we join the group in Baja as spring arrives and it is time to return to British Columbia to escape the extreme heat of the ten month long northern summer. Now everyone is on foot, no more motorcycles because they are out of gas.

On the way back they meet up with a whole bunch of characters who somehow survived the winter and who join them on their way to the cabin up north in BC.

When autumn comes along they all head south again and they meet up with several more people amidst more adventures.

By sheer luck they outwit the wiremen who are intending to ambush them and wipe them out. Instead they practically wipe out the wiremen but they lose a couple of people including Kacie's husband Mike.

The group gets split up and the second group try to follow behind the others. They eventually are reunited and everyone ends up safely back in Baja after some more adventures.

In book 3 "2020 Africa" several groups of people and children this time in Europe, start their journey away from the ice and snow of winter and into Africa in search of warmth. First the Sahara then darkest Africa and finally East Africa. After many adventures including climbing mount Kilimanjaro they end up in North America where they chance upon the original journey people and join up with them.

Now in book 4 it is 400 years after PJ, Kacie, Dale, Heather and Dee and all the rest of the friends and the bicycle crew from Europe and Africa first set out on their journeys. But our year is now 912 days long so 400 is a thousand of the old earth years. There are no months anymore, we don't need them. Our lives are governed by just days, seasons, years, and the ages of man. Our greatest civilization was reclaimed by the forests and deserts, and our buildings crumbled back into the dust and rock that they had always been.

Everything that ever happened to the early humans might as well never have happened at all, and time... their time, is all wrong now anyway. Only the day is the same, 24 hours, and the sunrise and sunset rules our lives once more like we had never left the great outdoors to live inside in the artificial light in the caves of our office blocks and apartments and the warehouses we called 'morls'. We used to travel from one cave to the other in 'horizontal elevators', vehicles that were so automatic we didn't have to think to drive them, and we didn't even have to know how to get anywhere with satellites that talked us to our destination or electric cars that drove themselves and recharged their batteries from the very roads they were driving on without stopping. So we sat back and read a book or watched a movie or played a game. Driving a vehicle wasn't a journey anymore, as long as you wanted to go where everyone else went. Cattle? Yes you could say we were cattle and it was progress in a way, but for the people who ran our countries rather than us. We still did what they wanted just like in the middle ages only now they knew where we were going and where we were all the time.

We were all part of a huge Supervisory Control and Data Acquisition mechanism (SCADA) that enabled our rulers to maintain, not just law and order, but control over our minds and thought. Control over what we thought we wanted and where we thought we wanted to go and what we wanted to do. As far as being free, that wasn't going to happen. All they had to do was shape our desires using the media in such a way that we always wanted something that was just beyond the reach of our wallets. We actually made it easy for them, we were all dreaming of making it big in the huge unofficial lottery that we were all entered in. All we had to do was be there and we could be one of the few who actually made it... the lucky rich winners of life, the ones who patented "the next big thing". Like all lotteries though it was one we could never win, but someone always knew someone who knew someone who had won. And that person was now living the 'good life' on some palm treed golden sand beach filled with permanent summer. As if the good life was any better than just life itself.

Through all our cycles of discarding the old and buying the new – better – improved – cleaner – more friendly – sleeker – sexier – more manly, and perhaps – less expensive, they tracked us. At the supermarket checkout: "Do you have your club card?" At the bank, well...of course. At the petrol station: Accepting all cards! Even at home... Save when you bundle your internet, phone and television. All tracked even the programs we watched on the telly. They knew everything, including our taxes. Oh yes they knew all about us. But the strange thing was... most of us didn't care. We fell for every glittering ruse, we bought in to every fast rush, each quick fix, the holiday we 'deserve', the kitchen we've 'always wanted', and every promise of a better easier tomorrow. Along the road every now and then, someone found a way to beat the system and trashed it all, and as our world collapsed, we the people sucked it in and moved on, or died. The beauty of it all was, *we wanted it*. Imagine that, the animals actually wanting to be locked up in the cage!

Almost everyone died so long ago that even I have a hard time remembering and I'm the keeper of the memories, I'm supposed to be the one who knows. How did we get here in the forest on foot with a bunch of bows and arrows and spears? Well it was the wars. Yes I know there were always wars, it was our nature to fight and destroy and rape and pillage and loot. But it seemed like perhaps a third of us were trying to kill the second third and vice-versa, while the final third were trying to keep everyone alive, I mean everyone even basket cases, come on guys there's such a thing as quality of life, get real. In all these shenanigans the only thing that all three thirds were doing that was the same, was screwing. The outcome, pretty predictably, was the more we multiplied the more we acted like rats locked in a cage too small, and thus the more we destroyed the natural order of things on our planet. Perhaps the mess we created *was* the natural order of things. But as we became better at doing everything we became too good at creating death. We could find and track a big horned sheep with a satellite, and then kill it from so far away the sound of the bullet smacking into its flesh just disappeared into the darkness of the universe. We could sit in an office in the pristine countryside of the wealthy half of North America and 'eliminate' problems on the other side of the world using our silent and hidden weapons in the sky. Just as long as we could image the problems on our computers at any rate. We humans were the top of the food chain and we became so dominant and so good at the destruction of our environment that we created the most terrible war of all. Everyone was invited and everyone came, willing or not. It couldn't have happened to a nicer species.

The trigger was a huge meteorite that hit somewhere north of India and touched off earthquakes along the fault lines of the world and this brought about massive ocean waves that swept across all the low-lying lands where most of us lived. But this meteorite was only a fragment of a massive piece of rock and debris about half the size of our moon that came out of the blackness of space and only just missed us. How did we manage to not see something as big as this coming? This huge nameless meteor came so close its gravitational force altered the earth's tilt and precession into a different future. A future where the year and the seasons are so long you either freeze or burn to your death if you try and stay in one place.

No one knew exactly who it was that sent that first missile armed with a nuclear warhead. It made no sound to the people at ground zero. One moment you were alive and the next you never existed. All that is known is that hundreds of nuclear missiles were launched and by the time the final one had hit its target, together with the change in the tilt of the earth we had destroyed ourselves.

With the seasons so long no-one can live through the winter up north or the summer down south, but you can live in the winter down south and the summer up north. Autumn and spring were still lovely and we could live through them... we just had to follow these two seasons as autumn moved south across the continent and spring moved north. So we, the journey people, survived by migrating every year following both autumn and spring. There was one other group of people, an anomaly, who somehow managed to survive staying in one place in caves with hot springs. These were the wiremen, our mortal enemies. We know almost nothing about them. But we see them on the journey south, once every year.

What fires up our lives now is making it through the 2000 mile journey twice each year. The journey is what makes us what we are. It provides all the challenge we need to remain sharp and fit and at the top of our game—because the stakes are so high. There's no second chance, you get it right first time every time, or you die. It's very simple, the tough and lucky survive and breed, it's the way it always was. One of our big failings used to be keeping ourselves alive regardless of cost... as if it makes any difference in the end how long you live and just when you die!

The seasons and years define our lives altogether slower and more simple now. Even death is simple but just like before, it comes so fast, before you ever know it. In the year 400 the seasons change so slowly that almost no one bothers to count the years anymore... You are alive, that is the only thing that matters now. You are alive.

Chapter 1, The Land of the Long White Cloud.

It was coming up to dawn on the hills near the Lonely Mountain. There was fog covering the valley bottoms but everywhere else was clear and the stars had faded from the eastern sky. There was murder afoot this morning as a group of men stood around a forest glade. Leading the group was a huge bear of a man whose name was legend in these parts... Blackheart. He had a bush of unkempt black hair underneath a headdress of two big bull horns adorned with numerous small animal skulls and eagle feathers set up in a rather untidy array. In his hand was a giant two bladed axe, the head resting on the ground. Like his warriors he was dressed in a patchwork of animal skins but with his great size he looked more like a mythical being come down from the upper reaches of the mountain tops. He stood a foot taller than any of his men, a group of fifty or so rather scraggly and unkempt ruffians who were standing around him in the trees on the edge of the forest glade. The fog was moving uphill towards them slowly and ever so quietly through the trees as if it knew that foul deeds were afoot. Somewhere hidden in the fog below there was a long line of journey people heading their way on their annual migration from British Columbia south to the sun.

Blackheart was annoyed. Actually he was more than annoyed. The feeling deep within him was truly nasty. Had he been a man of words he would have described his mood as blacker than the arse of a black bull in the middle of the darkest night of winter. But he was not into words, ever. When he was in this sort of mood, typically he killed something, preferably by hacking it into pieces so small they no longer resembled anything more than a bloody mess. The reason today for his bad mood was his mate Annie the Terrible had refused to let him call himself Blackheart the Bastard. "Other people can call you that out of respect but I mated with you because you were the meanest son of a bitch ever born. You are feared throughout all our people. Our greatest warrior, our greatest fighter, a natural leader of the wiremen. Blackheart is what our leader has always been called. You are known as Blackheart. That is enough."

Now the sun came up on the start of a beautiful autumn day and, still smarting from the argument, Blackheart went into battle with the journey people in this foul mood. He sliced and hacked his way through everyone near him, giving no quarter, radiating death and destruction so much that none of the other wiremen came close to him even when the fighting had ended.

Towering like the Lonely Mountain itself Blackheart stood there amongst the fallen and bloody bodies, his axe head sunk on the ground, his body slightly hunched forward, still wound like a clock spring. He felt like ripping the limbs off the dead journey warrior at his feet with his bare hands. Instead he snarled at the other wiremen around him, raised his axe over his head and sliced through the arm of the dead warrior beneath him at the shoulder. Then with a huge roar he hacked off one of the legs. Encouraged, everyone else started stripping the clothes off the bodies of the dead and hacking the bodies up, piling the assembled limbs and carcasses to be taken back to the mountain caves where they lived. This fresh meat would be stored in one of the ice caves. The 'Long Pig' as they called it would keep them alive through the short daylight and seemingly unending darkness of the bitterly cold winter. There were few other sources of food in the winter other than what they stored. They hunted and trapped game of course, but this was not enough on its own. The game seemed to pretty much disappear in winter.

Most of their time was spent in semi-hibernation in their caves. They were kept heated by warm springs bubbling out of the inner reaches of the mountains and passing through the caves into the whiteness outside. This formed small clear paths of steaming liquid that eventually trickled to a standstill in the snow and froze encased in wondrous formations of ice dams in the frozen black shadow and snow white winter-dead world of the forest where they lived.

Among the dead lying on the ground was a pretty young woman who looked as though she was still living, there was very little blood on her so she might have just been knocked out. What no-one knew was that she was still conscious but unable to move. Stunned she lay there on the ground as two wiremen approached her. Almost without thought she let her mind duck down and hide where it couldn't be seen. One of the men knelt beside her and held his head up against her chest. He said something and there was a conversation between the two that seemed to come from a long way away, so far away she couldn't understand the words. But the meaning was clear enough... one of them placed something soft under her head and she let herself drift into the safety and comfort of complete unconsciousness. She knew nothing bad was going to happen to her now.

How do women know these things? Well even men know but perhaps not so clearly, and anyway men are designed to die, not live.

Journey women were well regarded in the wiremen's society, by the men at any rate. They were tough, slim, fit and able to fight for what they thought was right. The wireman women tended to be stout and verging on fat. Good cooks though. Having a journey wife was pretty much the height of desirability for those wiremen who were not into cave fighting, dogball, and the other blood sports that made up the fun part of the winter for them.

This young woman was pregnant although it didn't show and when her child was born it was brought up as a slave doing all the menial and dirty jobs around the caves. It was always being treated badly and shouted at; with very little food, mostly scraps it could scavenge. Yes it was a tough life but the baby never knew any different and it grew up strong. It actually thought it's name was Hayou. Or for more formal occasions... Hayou Fuckhed. Yes it was a tough baby, strong and lean, able to roll with all the punches it took, and it took a lot of them. Able to survive in about the most hostile environment a young journey

3

warrior would ever encounter, the caves of their mortal enemy, the wiremen.

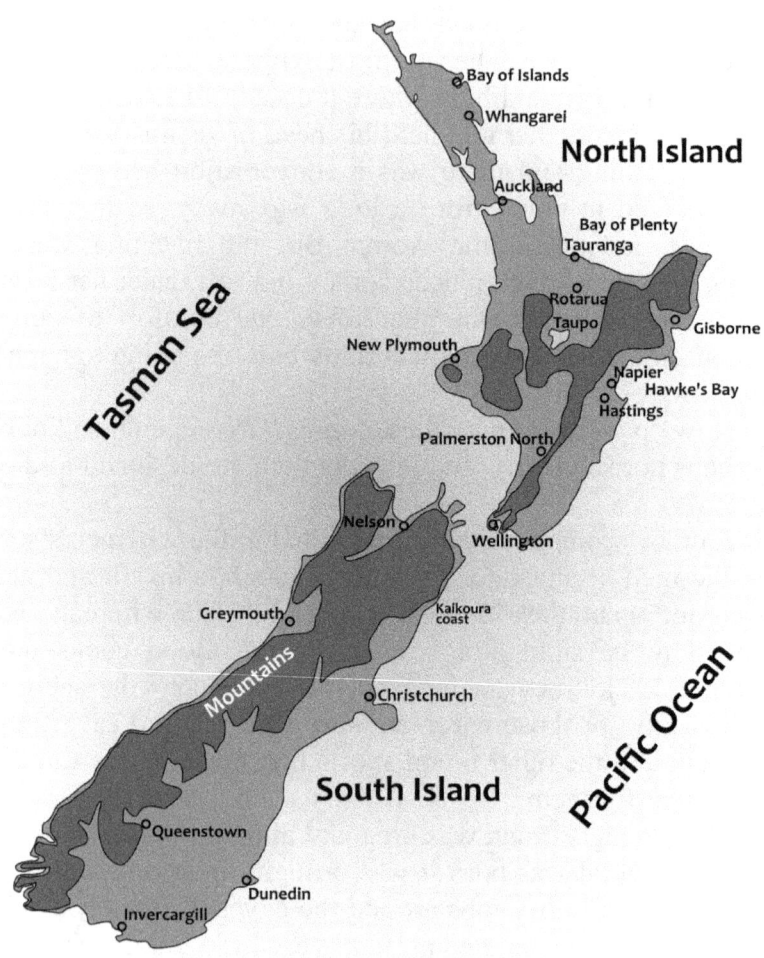

New Zealand before the meteorite hit north of India

Four hundred new years earlier and half a world away from the wiremen, Wally was down in the South Island of New Zealand in Invercargill visiting his brother when the meteorite hit up north of India and all hell broke loose in the world. Kiwi land was parked on the edge of the 'Pacific Rim of Fire', and of the earthquakes that devastated Japan, the far east and British Columbia all the way down to California and South America no place was harder hit than En Zed. In the South Island the main road that ran up the Kaikoura coast was obliterated by landslides and disappeared as the sea floor rose with the subduction of the pacific plate. The city of Christchurch effectively sank as the delta land liquefied and the ocean waves rushed in and then back out carrying man's puny dwellings with it. Fires and aftershocks finished the destruction off.

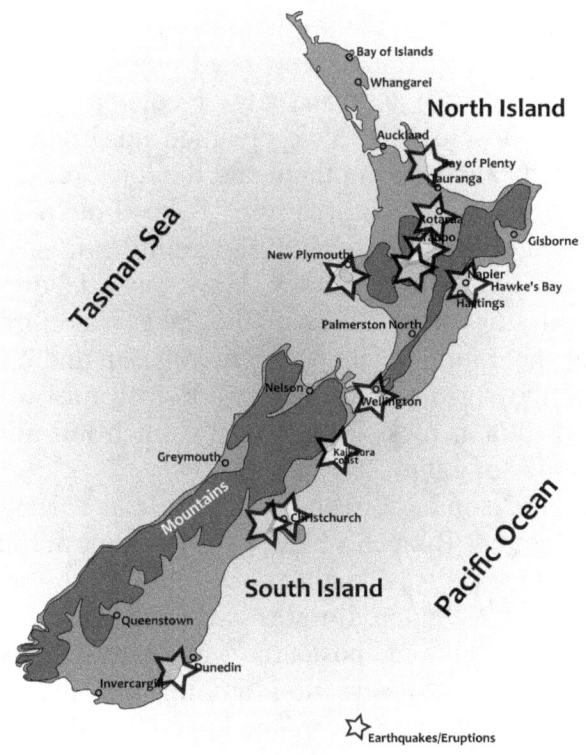

Post meteorite devastation

Up in the North Island on the east coast, Napier was flattened. All its prized Art Deco shop fronts from the

5

rebuilding after the devastating 1931 earthquake were pulverised and sank as the ocean flooded in. Most of the surrounding land was raised but in doing so the buildings of the suburbs on the land were crumpled into trash. The high ground of Hospital Hill and Bluff Hill was left isolated by rubble on the south and water on the north as a shallow lagoon formed all the way out to Taradale. The economically depressed area of Hastings was left above sea level, but the population of the prison, one of Hastings' few money spinners, was let loose on the streets after the power failed. New Zealand's criminals roaming the streets were the least of everyone's problems though.

Up north at Rotorua the tourist traps of natural steam geysers and bubbling hot mudpools expanded and agglomerated into a vision of hell worse than any medieval nightmare that Hieronymus Bosch could have dreamed up, ironically trapping all the tourists and burning them and the local residents, to their death. Just south of Rotorua was Lake Taupo. It was New Zealand's biggest lake, over 200 square miles in size and it was pretty much blown into the sky. How can a lake get blown—Boom—into the sky? Because the lake was formed in the caldera of the Taupo volcano which woke up and covered large chunks of the surrounding countryside in a mix of mud, dust, stones and molten rock. There wasn't much left alive within a hundred miles of Taupo.

Just to the south of what had been Lake Taupo the nine thousand foot Mt Ruapehu blew its top adding more chaos and helping to block all the main routes through the centre of the North Island. A hundred miles west of Ruapehu the eight thousand foot picture postcard Mt Taranaki also erupted, sending death and destruction among the sheep and cows grazing peacefully in the verdant lowlands all around it—and sweeping the city of New Plymouth into the sea under a huge flow of lava.

"Strewth mate we'll have to call it New Pompeii," said one local wag who survived because he had walked outside for smoko when he had finished milking and saw the pyroclastic flow start and head his way. He opened up a taranaki gate and made it safely past the silage pit and into the hills, driving what turned out to be one of the fastest Massey Ferguson tractors ever built, at least since the days of the Ferguson 4-wheel drive F1 racing car.

Even with all this going on Wally felt like it was a good idea to get home to the Bay of Islands up on the northern end of the North Island. He had a job as a tour guide with an adventure tour operator—jet skis, dune buggies, motor and sailboats etc; and he had a girlfriend up there. Actually the girl was the main reason! His brother tried to get him to stay, pointing out all the problems he would have with the reports of chaos on the Kaikoura coast and the general meltdown of civilization everywhere.

"The roads are impassable," his brother said. "You need a gyrocopter, not a motorbike. The middle of the North Island is a disaster area. They say Lake Taupo blew into the sky. Hey man, you can't get through. No one can get through!"

But Wally was a stubborn sort of guy and insisted that he would prefer to be up closer to the equator where it was reasonably warm rather than freezing his butt off in the coldest city in the country now that winter was on its way.

"There's no power here. You'll freeze."

"No. You're crazy. We're going to be fine. We can cut wood. It'll be like camping out."

"I don't mind camping out, but not in winter. And not with everyone else competing for wood. I'm going now while I can still get petrol. Pretty soon the stations will be sucked dry."

Wally was a short lad, about five foot six. slim and reasonably fit, but then he was in his early twenties and everyone his age jolly well ought to be fit. He had black, naturally curly hair and thick-rimmed glasses. Definitely a good looking sort of guy in a bookish way, plus he was smart. It was hard to one-up Wally.

He had a near vintage two-stroke 350 Jawa twin. It had a

huge three gallon petrol tank, standard issue for pre-glasnost Czechoslovakia in the 1960s back when the bike was made. Plus those Jawas and CZs the Czechs made were tough, they had to be tough to deal with the roads in Russia and the other eastern block countries in those days.

Wally's bro had one last try. "What if you run out in the sticks, what then?"

"I won't run out in the sticks, this thing gets incredible miles per gallon. I once went all the way from Castlepoint on the coast in the Wairarapa, back to Wellington on what was virtually an empty tank. All the way over the Rimutakas!"

Wally's 350 Jawa twin

"The Rimutakas aren't that high. But why on earth did you do that?"

"The Wairarapa closed down in the evenings back then, there were no petrol stations open. I just kept riding like I was on an economy run. I crouched down over the petrol tank to keep my wind resistance low and kept my speed down. I coasted down all the hills and used really gentle acceleration. Boring as hell and my hands froze but I got home! Actually I got stopped by the cops between Lower Hut and Wellington because I had my lights off."

"What?"

"My battery was running low and the engine needs the battery to get a spark. I could see well enough without lights. Hey there was nobody else on the road. I flipped them back on while the cops could see me and then back off again after I was out of sight. There's just too much regulation nowadays. There were street lights—of course I could see! Actually I could see better in the boonies where there was only starlight. You just adjust your speed and learn to read the road. Piece of cake." Wally was on a roll. "Well depth of field is not great because it's all shades of grey. But still, piece a cake. Didn't someone make a movie about racing a motorbike in the dark? What was it called... 50 Shades of Grey?"

"Right, you don't get out much do you! So what if your battery goes flat again?"

"Aint gonna happen again. Turns out the carbon pickup brushes in the generator had worn down. They were not touching the commutator properly. Simple fix—put new brushes in. They last forever anyway."

His brother didn't see the irony of that last statement. He just shrugged his shoulders and shook his head. There was no point arguing with Wally once he set his mind to it. He may be wrong but he was going to do it anyway.

Wally had salvaged the bike after a mate of his had given it to him so he could clear a bit of room in his shed. Wally couldn't afford a newer bike, he was a party guy and tended to spend his week's pay on a couple or three half-G's of beer and a feed of fish and chips. When the beer ran out... well it was time to go back to work. He was not exactly a career oriented type— he worked hard and he partied hard. But then so did everyone his age, New Zealand was not called 'Grogs own country' for nothing.

When he got the bike, the engine of the Jawa ran just fine, it was built like a tank, but the running gear, stuff like wheel bearings and cables... that all had to be replaced. The original Barum tyres were shot too, the Barums never were much good even when they were new. The chain was fully enclosed and in perfect condition along with the front and rear sprockets. He couldn't do anything about the worst part of the bike though. This was the combined left-side kickstarter, gear-shift, and supplementary clutch lever. To start the bike you pushed the lever in and it disengaged from shifting mechanism then you swivelled it back where it engaged the starter gears and you gave it a swift kick. When the engine started you swivelled the lever back to the gearshift position.

The clutch was disengaged in the gear-shift possie by an eccentric cam once you moved the lever up or down to change a gear, but this was just an emergency thing. Normally you used the clutch. It was all pretty nifty but if you needed to rattle your dags getting the shift from first to second—you could get neutral and a flapping kickstarter instead. Rather embarrassing if you were trying to beat an old lady in a wheelchair off the lights.

"You just want to get inside your girlfriend's pants," said Wally's bro, "that's the warm place you're looking for!"

"You're just jealous!"

"Yeah, well of course I'm jealous!"

"You want to come? I got a pillion seat. My girl has a sister, but she's a bit on the tubby side. Her family tend to go a bit pear-shaped as they age."

"No, I got things to do here, and there's a cute little sheila behind the bar at the pub, I think she's keen on me."

Wally was always half broke so his brother gave him several hundred dollars. "You can pay me back next time you see me."

"Yeah, and it'll be my shout down at the pub too. Look after yourself little brother and say hi to the sheila at the pub from me."

They hugged each other. "Hooray mate," said Wally's bro, "I'll see you next time you're down."

Wally took one last look at him, grinned and said "Yeah, hooray mate." Then he headed off inland because the main road on the coast was closed just before Dunedin. He filled up at Queenstown but was told the west coast road was closed by rock slides so he carried on inland heading for Arthur's Pass and Greymouth. It was 400 miles to Greymouth which he figured he could do on the full tank if he was real careful. He had a one quart bottle of petrol as an emergency spare.

When he got the other side of the hills he was struck by how empty everywhere was. There were very few survivors of the quake that hit the Kaikoura coast and the Christchurch area and there were still major after-shocks happening. He'd be puttering down the road minding his own business when the road would start to move and sometimes cracks would appear. "Weird. Bit like I've been hitting the booze on an empty stomach," he thought to himself.

Wally kept to the eastern foothills of the mountains which were the backbone of the South Island and he linked up with highway 73 at a small town which appeared deserted. It was kind of spooky. Perhaps everyone was keeping warm indoors... except there was no smoke coming from any of the chimneys. Heading up Arthur's Pass it started to snow. This pass used to be the southernmost road over the mountains to the west coast from Christchurch. There must have been someone ahead of him in a lorry and it was real treacherous for the Jawa where he had to slot in and out of the lorries deep twin tracks from the rear tyres.

Towards the top of the pass the tracks were mostly filled in with fresh snow but this didn't help at all, it was still tricky as all get-out trying to stay upright. The best place to be was in the virgin snow but the lorry kept going all over the place so he was forced to slot in and out of its wheel ruts and this meant all feet down trying to stop the bike falling over. Very tiring. Wally found himself wishing he could stop and warm up, with a beer of course.

Half way down the western side of the pass he met a grader operator in a government lorry getting set up to pull the lorry that had been ahead of Wally out of the ditch. The lorry in the ditch was an old flatbed with nothing on the bed so that was why it was going all over the place, no weight over the driving wheels. Wally stopped to help the grader driver get tied up. "Gidday mate, let me give you a hand!" As they were doing this an old VW Beetle came chugging down the pass and everyone stopped to chat. The family in the beetle were heading for

Towing out the stranded lorry at Arthurs Pass

friends in Greymouth and hadn't had any trouble in the snow. "Narrow tyres and the engine over the driving wheels," suggested Wally. "Knowing how to drive helps too!" said the driver's wife with a grin towards her husband who was looking quite chuffed with himself. Then they all travelled in convoy the rest of the way down the pass to where the grader was stored. The snow had disappeared by then and the flatbed lorry and the beetle carried on to Greymouth. Wally helped the grader driver get the chains off the lorry. The driver was just a young kid about the same age as Wally and invited him in to his place to warm up and grab a bite to eat and a beer. But best of all, he gave Wally a tank full of petrol on the house.

"There's none left in Greymouth. You may be OK in Nelson though. Worth giving it a try."

Later as they were chowing down he said: "I've got a few mates coming round for a bit a party tonight. You up for that?"

Wally was never one to shy away from a party.

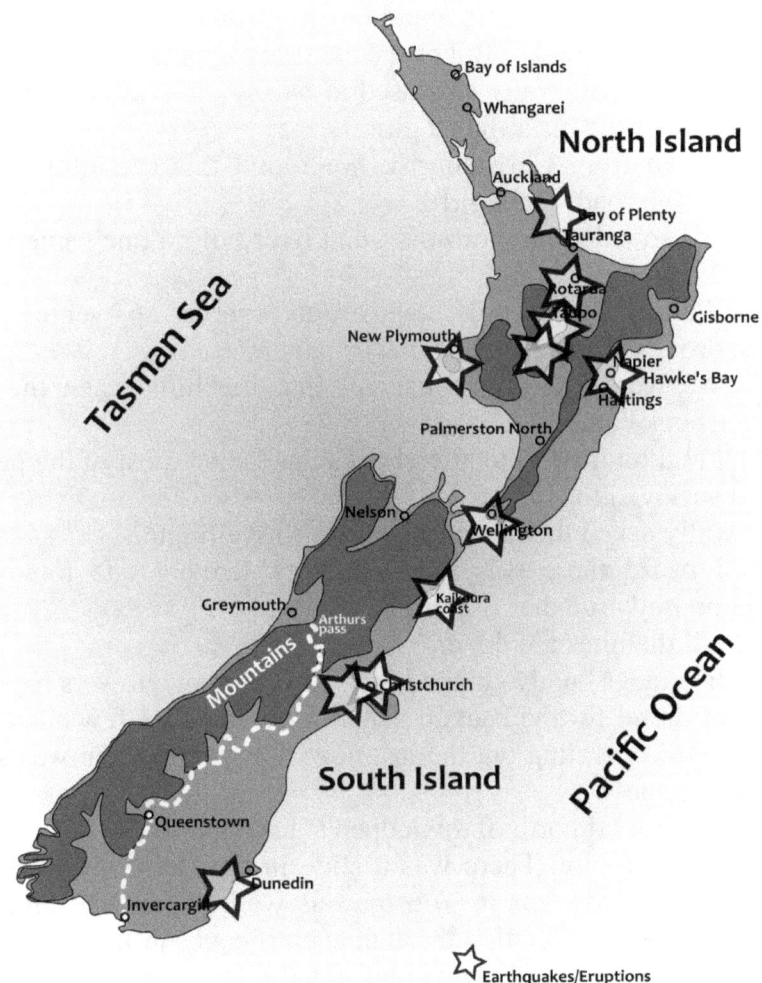

Day one

A few mates turned out to be a fair sized chunk of Greymouth's youth and while petrol was in short supply booze was definitely not. On the surface the party seemed fine, lots of kids were getting drunk and there was a lot of noise so you had to shout at someone standing next to you if you wanted to be heard. But there was an edge to the laughter and the smiles seemed a little too wide to be real. Some of the faces of the girls had eyes that seemed to stand out from their makeup as if they were wearing masks. But everyone was too drunk to notice little things like that. Wally was used to booze and was chatting with a couple of the mask-faced girls.

"We're from Christchurch. We found this car idling at the side of the road," said girl 1.

"We sounded the horn over and over but no one came," said girl 2.

"Well we couldn't just stand around forever, so eventually we just drove off and headed here."

"We were lucky, we just got into the hills when the first aftershock came."

"I reckon it was the aftershocks that killed most of the people that survived the quake."

Wally asked them about the ferry to Wellington.

"I heard there was one last ferry leaving late tomorrow. Dunno how true that is though."

"All the lines are down."

His grader buddy chipped in: "The cellphone towers have run out of diesel for the backup generators. There's a few ham radio guys still operating but the last news I got from them was some time ago now."

"Is the road north of town open?" asked Wally.

"I'm not sure. There was a slide in the Buller Gorge. They were trying to clear it. You may as well go. On the bike you have a chance of getting through even if cars can't."

So Wally bunked down and got a couple of hours rest and took off for Nelson early the next morning to try to make the ferry.

About 40 miles after Greymouth he was passing through a small village when a flock of geese ran out in front of him and he couldn't avoid ploughing into them. They thumped and banged and squawked as they tumbled under the bike and then the banging stopped. He carried on and didn't look back. There was nothing he could do to help the geese.

True enough there was a slide in the Buller Gorge with several empty cars parked along the side of the road together with an abandoned bulldozer. "Probably out of diesel," he thought. But as his grader friend had suggested there was enough room for a motorbike to get through by dodging around the boulders and rocks still littering the road.

In Nelson he filled up though he had to buy premium because they were out of regular. He was chundering along just fine the other side of Nelson and he was feeling good about getting to the ferry when he got a puncture. It took him forty minutes and a lot of swearing to get the wheel and tyre off and the inner tube patched. And another ten to get it back on the bike and get going again. Now his hands were oily and his clothes dirty and he was rushing... using big handfuls of throttle to accelerate, cornering hard and going as fast down the straights as the twin two-stroke would go. He couldn't afford the time to save petrol anymore.

As he rushed flat out in to the ferry terminal he could see the ferry casting off but he squeezed the little Jawa by the barriers and headed up the wharf. The guy on the wharf waved him on while the guy in charge of the loading ramp on the ferry yelled and waved to him to get on the gas. He accelerated and rode up the moving platform as the gap between the boat and the wharf grew wider. His front wheel popped into the air as he cleared the ramp and there was a cheer from the passengers standing amongst their cars as he rode over and parked the bike. Wally went over to the guy who had waved him on board and gave him a high five.

"Jeez mate, that was close!"

"You're a regular hot-dog kid!"

"I am so glad to make this ferry. I heard it was the last one!" said Wally with a grin.

"I figure it's gonna be the last one for a while at any rate.

We've only got enough diesel for one run."

On the journey across the strait the talk was about Wellington. Large parts of it had been pretty much demolished by the quake and the aftershocks, the airport was unusable and there was only a single lane open out of the downtown area heading inland. Plus there was a large prehistoric monster from the props department at the Stone Street film studios that had been relocated so it was greedily towering over the "Wellington" sign on the hill at Miramar facing the harbour... but not a 'varsity student or camera and sound man in sight.

"Who would spend their time doing a prank like that?" said a passenger.

"You gotta have a sense of humour," replied Wally. "The end of the world and some guys still have time for a laugh. Works for me. Are there many people still around?"

"The place is pretty much deserted," said one of the crew members. "Not quite sure what I'm going to do. Might stay with my sister in Upper Hutt."

Docking at Wellington harbour should have been easy but it was dark when they got there (no electricity in the city of course) and there were no dockworkers to tie up the ship. The captain advised everyone to leave by the car deck so Wally was lined up at the front of all the foot passengers with the big two-stroke ticking over quietly while the cars waited behind them all. As the wharf moved closer in the rather ominous flares of light from the ship's spotlights there was a ripple through the crowd. Everyone was nervous like it was the start of a race.

Several of the crew leaped on to the dock as the ferry touched the wharf and they loosely wound the mooring ropes to bollards. Then the ramp slammed down and Wally was off like a long dog onto the wharf and into town. Just then another aftershock hit and the ferry was partially toppled as the wharf started collapsing. Wally was concentrating on getting to the highway out of town that ran alongside the harbour and didn't hear the screams as the passengers and vehicles were sucked off the wharf into the icy cold waters.

The highway up over the hill to Palmerston North was blocked by barricades, obviously it was impassable so he

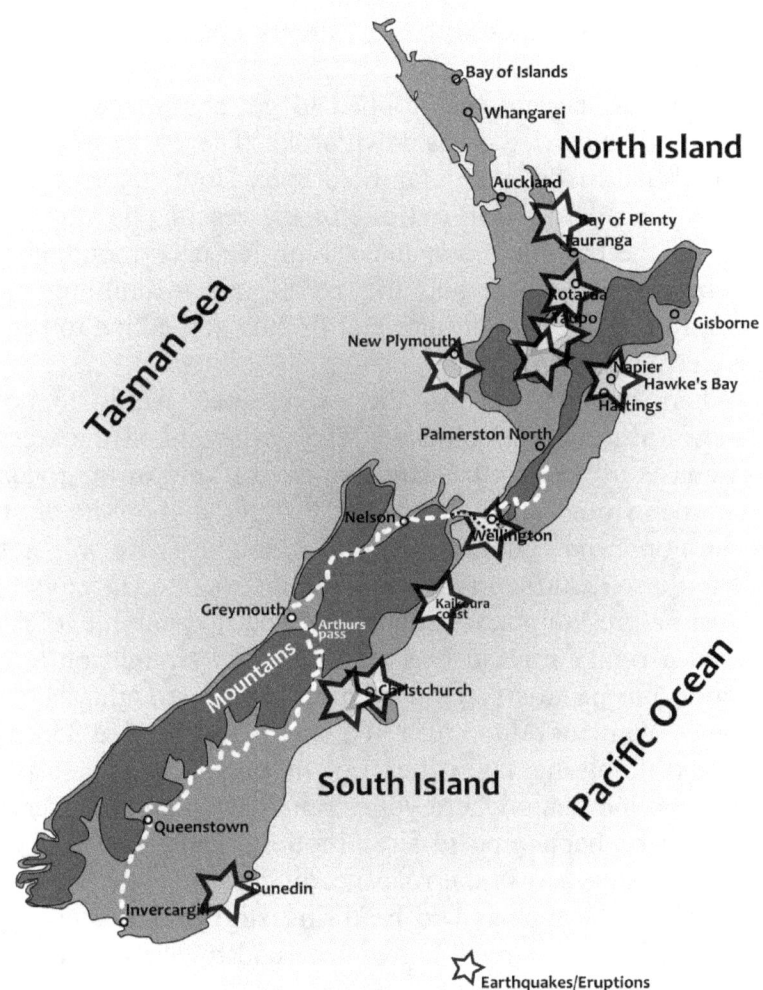

Day two

carried on to Lower and Upper Hutt and on up the long climb to the top of the Rimatukas. It started to snow a bit up towards the top but not enough to slow Wally down. The snow stopped as he got down into the Wairarapa on the other side. All the little villages including the main town of Masterton were completely dark and asleep as he headed north into the early morning. It was weird passing through the dark stop lights in the silent black and grey ghost towns with side streets that now might just as well have gone nowhere at all.

Out in the country he stopped to get some sleep in an old barn and then carried on as dawn broke. There was freezing rain and hail that made Wally numb all over. Hours later he stopped to take a pee and found out one of the reasons he was so cold was that the hail had compacted to an ice pack moulded to the gap between his legs and the petrol tank—fumbling around under all the layers of clothes and finding something to pee with was a real problem!

When he got out of the Wairarapa, Wally found the Manawatu gorge was blocked. The gorge linked the west and east coasts of the North Island. So even if any of the roads had been open from Palmerston North to Auckland on the west side of the gorge, he couldn't have got through. There was nothing else to do so he turned right and took the road to Hawke's Bay.

Just before Waipukurau he made a really dumb move. He had missed a right turn and was starting to go straight on at a 'Y' junction but he was so cold he didn't think straight and turned anyway. You can't do U turn in a single lane road at 35mph. So the next thing he knew he was in one of those suspended animation moments where your brain speeds up and everything seems to be happening in slow motion... There he was on the ground sliding across the road heading straight for a telephone pole. The pole appeared to be tilting slightly left then slightly right as his head banged across the road but he couldn't move his arms to protect himself and there was nothing he could do to miss—whump—he and the bike hit the ditch on the edge of the road and everything, both slow and fast, stopped moving. The ditch had stopped him hitting the pole. Phew! He picked himself and the bike up, dusted himself down checked the clutch and brake levers and carried on. This time on the right road. Good job those Jawas are so solid—there was nothing wrong with the bike and all the clothes he was wearing meant there was nothing wrong with him either. But now he was fully awake again!

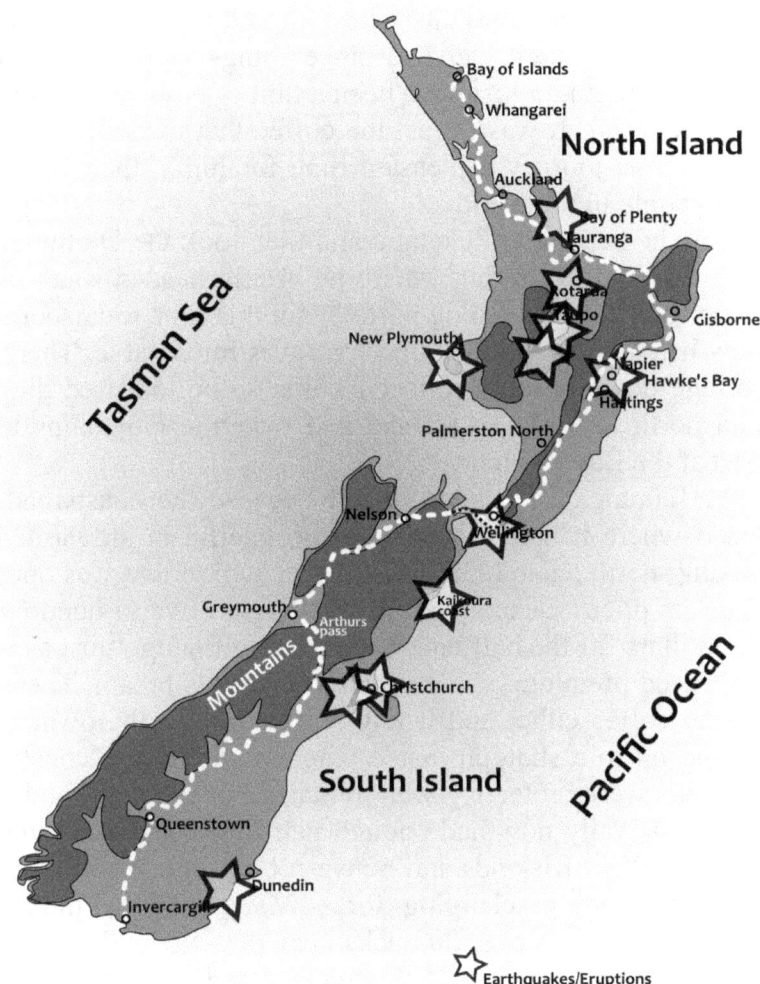

Day three

When he got to Waipawa there was a partial barrier across the road and a sign warning of the trouble ahead in the delta lands where the cities of Napier and Hastings were. So he hung a left and then took the road to Fernhill. He knew he had to avoid Napier and Hastings anyway. Somewhere in all these back roads Wally found a petrol station open and filled up. The husband and wife team that owned the station shared their early morning coffee and biscuits with him and they talked about all the hard times they had had since things went bad with the world. There might just have been a hint of envy in their eyes as Wally rode off. It wasn't just the coffee that made the next few hours of the journey a pleasant time for him... there were still good people in the world.

Now he headed to Puketapu and then took the Dartmoor and Pukititiri road to Eskdale where he briefly headed south on the Taupo road before heading north again this time to Gisborne, he knew heading north the Taupo road was impassable. There was a bridge down heading in to Gisborne so he followed the river delta north towards Te Karaka and over the mountains to the coast at the Bay of Plenty.

At Tauranga he headed inland because the coast road was closed where it had slipped into the Pacific in an earthquake. Heading north again he found a petrol station that was open but it had its prices jacked way up. Wally paid over a hundred and fifty dollars for the half tank he needed to top up. "Just as well I don't need premium," he grumbled under his breath. There was no free coffee either and it looked like one of the owners was holding on to a shotgun inside where some hastily constructed steel bars were protecting what remained of the junk food in the shop. But Wally now had enough petrol to get him all the way up to the Bay of Islands and he wasn't big into junk food. "Not sure what they're charging for a Mars bar," he thought to himself, "but if it's over 20 bucks I can do without."

Auckland was a mess with wrecks littering all the highways, but he expected that and took off to the west towards Parakai and rejoined the main highway half a day later. At Whangarei there was a huge pall of dirty black smoke coming from the oil refinery. "Something must have caught fire in one of the tanks," thought Wally. "Or maybe a tank split and the contents soaked into the ground and caught fire." It was less than 100 miles now and already he was looking forward to the great food his girlfriend Rangi seemed to rustle up out of nothing.

"Bet you're ready for a feed," was the first thing she said as she hugged him. "and a shower too." she added letting him go and wrinkling her nose!

Twelve months later, after the end of winter, Wally and Rangi crewed up with a small flotilla of yachts that set sail to Invercargill in late spring to see if they could keep a bit cooler down south in the summer.

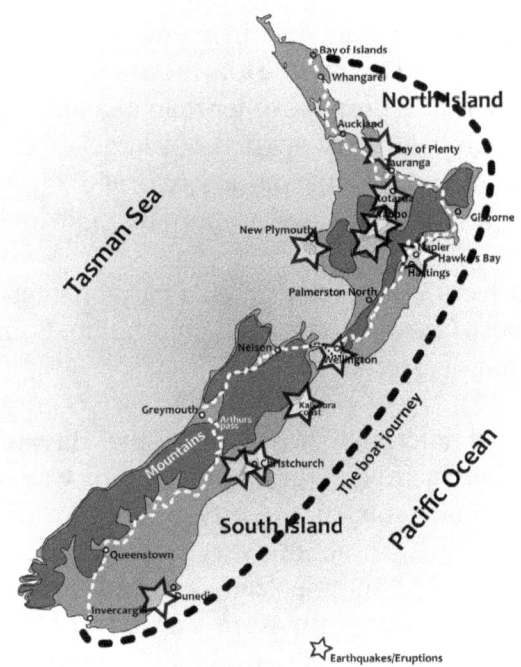

The boat journey back to Invercargill

"This is a good way for us to live gal, I think we're going to be among the few who survive this mess. In the short term anyway."

When they got there, Wally's bro had disappeared without trace. There weren't many other people around either, not alive anyway. Just a whole bunch of corpses mostly holed up inside houses where they had frozen to death.

Wally and Rangi and the other sailors had to work pretty much dawn to dusk growing food. "This is not as easy as it looks," said Wally, "You don't just make a hole in the ground and put a seed in it."

"Keeps us busy though," added Rangi. "Remember back in the day how we always had to be doing something, working, playing, going somewhere else just because we'd never been there. Our lives were like the cartoons on the telly we watched as kids... the cartoons were always changing, something on the face moving, an eyelid, a different camera perspective— panning, zooming. The picture on the screen never stayed still but frequently for no purpose other than change itself. And when there was a purpose it was spelled out large—exaggerated even if it was as inconsequential as a yawn and this made the big things seem less big and less important. 'Oh look the cartoon moved—wow.'"

"Yes, our lives were pretty much a cartoon back then. We had no real purpose. Now I don't need entertainment in the evening. All I want to do is sleep."

Three years later the crowd from the Bay of Islands had summered over in Invercargill again. There was no one left of the original inhabitants of the city now. The three ten month winters had turned just about everything organic into blocks of ice each winter until summer came around. It was now autumn and the cold antarctic winds were starting to blow up from the Ross Sea. Invercargill was the southernmost city in New Zealand and actually quite liveable in the heart of the ten month long summer. Wally and Rangi and the boat people had grown a good stock of food including long-lasting items like grains and seeds, but had also preserved things like tomatoes in jars. Stuff that would keep while they made the trip north and waited for their winter crops to reach harvest.

As they got ready to ship out the owner of the biggest yacht

22

said: "This is it guys, we can't just do the easy trip up to the Bay of Islands this year."

"Why not?" asked Rangi.

"It's been getting worse each year. Winter up there is just too bloody cold. We nearly froze last year, you remember? Pretty soon our crops won't have enough time to grow. Basically we're screwed. We're going to have to go further north this year."

"Rarotonga?"

"Up into the central Pacific and whatever works. I think we ought to stay away from the bigger islands just in case anyone survived. You never know, they used to be cannibals."

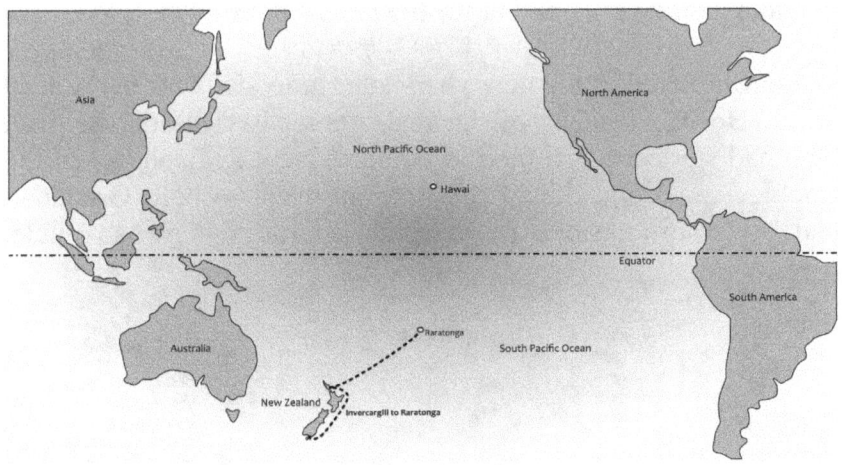

Looking for warmth in winter in Rarotonga

"I must admit I'm partial to a bit of 'long pig' every now and then!" replied Rangi.

Wally gave her a strong push on the shoulder. "That's disgusting gal."

"That is not the 'Long Pig' I'm referring to!" And she grabbed him 'round the waist and wriggled her body up against his crotch.

Wally got it... "Oh you can have a bit of that 'long pig' anytime gal!"

"Coming back here for summer is going to be a bitch," said

the owner. "Rarotonga is a long way to sail. We gotta do it though. At least the yachts are good for a few more years. Actually a few more lifetimes."

"Yeah, then what?" said Wally.

"Who cares. The grandkids can figure it out. That's their problem!"

"With any luck," said Rangi, "it'll be the great grandkids and we'll all be long gone." And she kissed Wally.

So the small flotilla of yachts set sail for the Cook Islands after refilling their water tanks at Whangarei. There the oil refinery was still burning deep down in the ground.

They didn't know it but long sea journeys was what they would become very good at for the rest of their lives.

Four hundred of the new years later granddad was in the lead yacht. He was the last of the really great navigators, the ones who had started out in the old country, New Zealand, when the troubles came and the worlds seasons went to hell. Granddad had been born on one of the great journeys they had made.

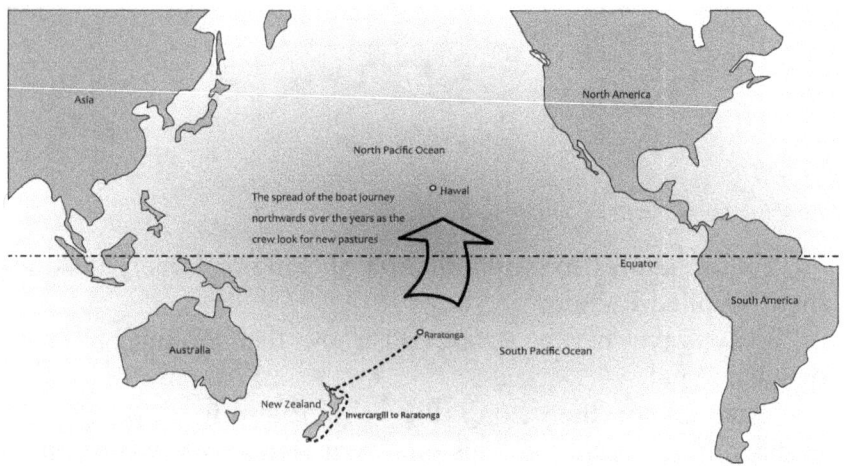

Heading for new pastures

These journeys spanned over half of the Pacific and granddad had learned his navigating skills well. He could take them across this vast empty ocean without stars and without tools and get them to the landfall they needed. Just by reading the waves he could hit a small island hundreds of miles away in the featureless expanse of the great Pacific ocean. Now he was 38 (95 of the old earth years) or thereabouts, no-one really knew for sure.

As the ages rolled by and the generations changed, their people had been heading ever northward on the northern leg on their journeys from the southern tip of New Zealand. Now he knew he was making his last journey and he had a deep inner sense of peace, of arrival, something was telling him this would be the last of the great sea journeys.

He was sitting at the stern in the lead yacht when one of his grandkids yelled out.

"There's a cloud, there's land ahead!"

It was some time before granddad could see the cloud, his eyes were not so good now. By then the cloud was covering nearly the whole of the horizon ahead just over the bow to the east, and they could smell the deep musky scent of land.

"It's the land of the long white cloud," said the old man.

"The one they talk about in the stories?"

"Yep, this is it. There's water and animals to hunt. And fruits and berries."

"Good-Oh. Water, food and land; it's all we need. We can live there," said his great granddaughter holding her new baby in her arms.

They sailed in to a big inlet 10 to 15 miles wide and over 50 miles deep and as they got farther away from the mighty Pacific the swell eased and a calmness began to descend on the small flotilla of yachts. The yachts all looked a bit of a mash-up... after a thousand of the old earth years cruising the Pacific they were now a patchwork quilt of repairs on the hulls and the sails were all hand sown out of whatever natural materials they could find. They looked on their last legs and not at all the sort of thing to be trusting your life to. But hey, what else to do? This was their life.

Almost mesmerized by the sight of land they glided past

dozens of islands with tall dark green fir trees growing right down to the water's edge, sometimes seeming to be growing straight out of the sea. They followed the light wind until they came across a peaceful flat shore on the mainland that had a beautiful sandy beach.

Dark green fir trees growing right down to the water's edge

At the stern of the lead yacht granddad Wally smiled, he knew he had arrived.

Chapter 2, Autumn in the Wild.

Way up high in a mountain valley in central British Columbia the first leaves of autumn were falling. It seemed to Nawo that it was far too early for this to happen. Yesterday had almost felt as hot as the hottest day of summer in the afternoon and evening and even on into the night. Hot and muggy, not at all the right conditions to rest and sleep. The leaves stopped falling as if they had seen him looking at them but then an invisible puff of air gently touched midway up the trees and a half dozen more leaves fluttered to the ground.

As he looked up and down the valley Nawo could see other figures standing alone like him, or in small groups just looking at the day; all of them with spears and bows. He felt good, they were waiting, waiting for him to lead them south. Up towards the head of the valley on a ridge in the open was a dot. He could tell from the way the dot was standing it was Dee-an. Dee-an was his best scout and one of their best marksmen with a bow. Nawo smiled slightly and he knew that way up there almost out of sight on the ridge Dee-an was looking at him and smiling too. Nawo raised his spear above his head and so did Dee-an. They both knew, now was the time to leave. Nawo looked away, it was a bit chilly in the pre-dawn air, but the sun would be up high in a few more hours, then it would become too warm before they even realized it. His son Narok joined him and when Nawo looked back up the valley, Dee-an had gone from sight.

It was time to leave. Shinsum knew it in her heart, she could feel it in the air. There was a sharpness in the morning when you woke up and a certain delicate smell when you first walked outdoors that came only in the cooler days of mid autumn. The smell was cold and like not quite ripened fruit, crunchy, sharp and bitter-sweet. A smell to the air like no other. It was the smell of change. "Come," she said to her daughter Shiwobi. "We must go now, the days are getting short." She lifted her pack to her shoulders and Shiwobi lifted hers. She could see her mate Nawo was waiting on the other side of the clearing with their son Narok.

As Shinsum moved towards them she smiled, Nawo looked every bit as fine as the day she had first seen him. Tall and slim like his spear, his bow loosely strapped to one side of his pack his arrows in a pocket on the other side.

Nawo looked back and saw her move towards him with Shiwobi and he thought to himself: "Damn, she looks so good. Tough as nails, firm-bodied and still slim even after two kids." It was time. He knew that. He could feel it coursing through his body and sending every nerve upon an edge and glowing with a fire. It was time again to go south. Everything was in play. The journey had begun.

Nawo is tall, just over six feet. Slim but sturdy. He doesn't say much, he's quiet and tends not to get involved in what everyone else is talking about. But he's always aware of what's going on around him in the bush; the bundu is what he listens to. He notices movement and changes at the edges of the world around him, the places where the savannah meets the thick forest, or where the darker patches of the shadows meet a splash of sunlight in a clearing. He notices the junctions between the bushes and the open ground, and the play of light within the shrubs and brambles and tall grass at the time of seeding. He sees the hiding places in the foot of cliffs and he sees into the shadows in-between the rocks. Rocks covered in moss, or bare and brightly open to all the harshness of the seasons. He is somewhat distant from those people around him and he lives in the faint blue haze of an early summer day at the base of the foothills of the distant mountains in his mind.

Shinsum was a little shorter than Nawo. Slim and like all the journey people, fit and tough. You have to be tough to live in these times. Her daughter Shiwobi was six years old and on the verge of becoming a woman. Soon she would be seeking a mate. Shiwobi is slim and beautiful like her mother but she has her father's natural ability with finding her way in the bundu. Like all children her age she has a natural toughness that lets her do practically anything that has to be done.

Narok was seven, a young warrior, tall, tough and quiet like his father. When something has to be done he doesn't talk about it, he just does it and generally does it well. As with his father he likes being on his own, but alone or not, all the young women his age had big eyes for him.

There was no pre-set time to leave on the journey but somehow everyone knew, like the cherry trees all blossoming at the same time in spring, it must be something in the air.

Cherry blossoms

They were a very confident group these journey people. The way they carried themselves and the way they looked about them said everything you needed to know: They knew what they were doing. But they needed to be confident to set out on

29

foot on a two thousand mile migration twice each year.

As Nawo and his family travelled south other families were waiting in the shade of big old trees or moving in lines snaking down into the valley to join them. It was a bit chaotic in the first couple of days, there were old friends with stories to catch up with and new ones with bright expectant looks on their faces. It all took time to sort out until after a week, there was a stream of people behind Nawo, building into a huge river of families stretching back for miles and miles; a line several days long.

Nawo was a Master Guider, he knew the way and if it was blocked, he knew what to do, he knew where to go to get by. Without thinking, everyone followed, they knew, it was the way. At night their fires sprinkled across the blackness of their starlit world. Wisps of smoke and the smells of good cooking danced through the valleys and over the hills. Food and friendship was shared from fire to fire; they all knew that they would need each other, and that some of them would not get through to the wintering lands. Death was always with them on the journey. Not hidden, simply walking alongside them as their partner in life.

Today as they stood resting by the path, all about them it rained leaves amongst the rain as a light gusty wind blew around. The leaves were like giant yellow snowflakes whirling dodging swirling and spreading out, escaping from the tree at last and trying to get as far away as possible, as if they were in a competition to see who could go furthest in their freedom. The light rain came to an end and the gusts died down so that only a few leaves were left fluttering to earth. Even as many leaves as had fallen still left the trees bright yellow ochre against the dark black green of the firs behind in the elder forest. But now the path beneath their feet was yellow ochre too.

Life was pretty simple once the journey had begun. It took a day or so to sort everything out, but then the path was trodden down, bypasses or simple bridges made, shelters built, and a good place to hunt was passed on down from family to family, and everyone wherever they were in the line travelled like they were an extended family. Whenever anyone returned to the family group from a hunt or from helping out building bridges or making old trails passable they were greeted like long lost friends. Even a few hours absence was enough to trigger a wave of hugging, kissing and petting. It all served to keep the group together and bind them in the best possible way to ensure the safety and survival of all the journey people and their way of life.

After three weeks they crossed a spectacular landmark... the natural bridge over a huge river in the canyon, with the water tumbling away hundreds of feet below them. The path now led to the north west delta lands and the line of families stretched for over 90 miles, two to three days walk even on the easiest going.

Beorn had to rest, he had been falling behind his family for days, only catching up at night in time for the food they saved for him before they slept. At five and a half feet he is stocky and short but he is tough for his age. He has a craggy face, thinning white hair and a full white beard. He was a great fighter in his younger days and still retains some skill with a bow and sword, and he knows he is close to the end of his life. Beorn knew he wouldn't be eating with his family this night. His family knew that as well and had said goodbye in the morning. As they left he huddled by the fire still unrested from the day before. His body didn't work well enough for the journey now, his legs had stiffened, the muscles ached and hurt when he stretched and used them, and there was frequent sharp pain in the back of his legs either side of his knees and in the muscles alongside his hips. This forced him to stop or hobble along using a stick to prop himself up until the pain went away, although it never fully went away. Occasionally his knees or one of his hips gave way for no reason and he fell to the ground. Now he accepted the help of those around him to stand up. He wouldn't have done so even as little as five years ago, he was so fiercely independent.

31

He walked with a stoop but every so often he would remember the old men he had seen when he was young. How bad they looked as they shuffled along, all bent over looking down almost directly in front of them, and not seeing or caring about the beauty of the world around them. When they stopped and looked up they were talking to themselves and not seeing or listening to anything else at all. At the times when he thought about those old men, Beorn straightened his back and looked up as he walked. But it never lasted. The next time he thought about it he was stooped over again, it just felt more natural now. Besides it helped to keep the weight from his pack more forward.

Now he was always cold as the wind dried the sweat from his body when he stood still waiting for the pain to let him walk again.

All this was to be expected though, he was nearly thirty four and the oldest man by far this year.

As the days went by he dropped further and further back, helped with food by every family he was with at the evening fire. If only he could make the coastal plains before he got to the end of the line. On the plains he could keep up, perhaps even get back to his family. It would be so nice to share the first evening with the scent of salt water and seaweed near the ocean with his new son. It would be almost like making it to the wintering lands. On the natural bridge he looked back down into the valley and he could see the last people in the line. These were the weakest ones, the ones least likely to get through the journey south.

There was one more big valley and one more big range of hills before the plains. He sat down on the other side of the bridge to rest.

In the evening he was with Junga and Mace, old friends whom he had helped get through the badlands and north to the summer lands when they were still young children. Their parents had died there in the barren wastes of those badlands many years ago. The rains had not come and so many people had died that year.

In the morning it was still dark when everyone got up, and one by one the morning fires lit up dotting the hills and valleys with flickering smudges of gold and reddish light. Junga and

The Natural Bridge

Mace and their young children Alex, Alesis, and Flower split most of Beorn's pack amongst themselves leaving him only his weapons. Like Beorn, Junga and Mace were shorter than average. Junga was about five and a half and Mace a little less, but both were very fit and tough. Junga was always on for a long difficult trek to find food and it always seemed he could outlast anyone else, setting the pace uphills and never showing any fatigue despite his age. When Mace came hunting with them she was always up with Junga, and if Junga held back slightly so she could keep up—well everyone else was just too tired to notice.

There were times when Junga and the two oldest kids came back from a really tough long hunt late in the evening, so late they might not have been coming back at all—but Mace never showed any concern on her face. She and Flower had food waiting for them and a fire to relax by as they eat and warmed up. Everyone of the journey people took care of their family group but none more so than Junga and Mace. They always seemed to have extra time for each other and their kids, sometimes they spent hours doing nothing but playing and singing until everyone was all played out. So the house didn't get cleaned that day, or the beans weeded, or maybe it was a bit of pot-luck that evening. Well, hey—most of all that other stuff can be done tomorrow. Today is for us.

With only his weapons to carry and his heart lighter and body warmer Beorn walked on keeping up with everyone now as they climbed the last tall hills before the delta plains. That night they were at the top of the westernmost end of the hills and there was a sprinkling of snow on the ground. It was still the middle of autumn but the snows come early up this high. The small fires of the other families swept away from them downhill into the long valley that led to the delta plains. He had made it this far, now Beorn knew, he was going to make it to the sea.

Why did they go near to the sea? Was it some long forgotten call? It would seem to make more sense to take the shorter route inland. Well along the way there was the promise of an easy harvest. The salmon runs were awesome, more food than anyone could imagine using. There were several areas with permanent traps that were set by the scouts of Nawo's lead group. So that by the time everyone arrived at each location there were fish to harvest. The last families in the line removed the stakes that set the traps after they had made use of the bounty, thus preventing any more fish from being caught. Bears were sometimes a problem but in general they kept away from such a large group of people. If there was a problem... well bears were good meat too.

But the main reason to stay away from the inland plains as much as they could was the possibility of an early snowfall. If the snows came to the plains inland in autumn, there was a good chance they wouldn't leave and whiteness would cover everything on the earth in a blanket deeper than even the tallest man while lying down—until the start of spring came calling. But young spring was then far older than their memory would be frozen in the snow inland in the sparkling fresh new year.

Chapter 3, Gidday mate!

Beorn got all his stuff together and said goodbye to Junga and Mace and their children, and walked on to where his family were near the head of the line. He caught up to them while they were still at the second salmon traps. At the traps everyone rested and rebuilt their strength for however long it took to catch and smoke the salmon. He had reached them in just over a day. His family had almost finished resting so he helped harvest as much as he could carry before leaving with them to cross the delta and follow the lowland coastal plains towards the northern half-life lands.

They travelled to the east of the main river on a wide delta plain. Here there were many smaller streams and rivers and by criss-crossing the land they were able to use the few bridges still standing that had been built by the early humans. One of these bridges led them quite close to the sea and Beorn took his family and several others on a short diversion to the water's edge. They bathed in the salty water and the children made castles in the golden sand helped by Beorn. Time seemed to stand still for a few short hours. The adults watched or joined in the children's games and the children's voices rose up shouting and squealing in delight as they ran over the sand and through the small waves at the waters edge.

But at this point a most amazing thing happened... Several yachts appeared sailing up what had once been called Boundary Bay. In all the years of their lives they had been walking on the journey this had never happened before. The children stopped playing and everyone stood up and stared in wonder as the yachts silently got closer. Then they could see the crews standing on the bows and leaning out from the sides over the water holding on to ropes and staring right back at them. Twenty or thirty feet out the yachts raised their centreboards and let their sails go slack and they coasted silently in to ground their hulls on the beach. The sailors jumped off and waded towards the journey people helping granddad Wally to be first up the beach to meet Beorn.

"Gidday mate!" said Wally with a grin.

They all stayed at the beach that evening and had several fires and the best feast anyone could ever remember.

The next day the sailors got all their gear together and Beorn led everyone back to the main trail refreshed and smiling, and they started walking towards the northern half-life lands again. But they were walking slower now so as to let the legs of the sailors toughen up and that evening when they all stopped and the other families joined them there was a lot of explaining to do and stories to be told and retold!

Now they were heading inland to avoid the northern wastelands—the northern half-life lands. You could not go too close to this place that had once been a giant city. What had been carved out of the flood plains by the early humans was now once more just flood plains and swamps. Above the swamps almost nothing grew, just bare earth and rock and ruins, with black slime in the gullies in-between the ruins. There was life in this blackness, but it did not look with eyes like ours. It was said awful things would happen to you if you tried to walk through that terrible place. The journey people had to take to the foothills on what had once been a wide pathway, it was still paved in places but mostly it had all but disappeared with rock slides and washouts, and like everything else everywhere it had become overgrown with trees and plants only a few dozens of years after the end of all the nuclear missiles. Now the trees had matured and life had returned to normal under their canopy. The awesome ancient rainforests of the Pacific Northwest had returned.

If you were a Master Guider like Nawo you could see the way, even though there was nothing left on the plains or in the valleys. In these places at least once in every lifetime the major floods washed almost everything away. Even though there was no obvious direction to follow Nawo could see which way to head by following his instincts and his feelings. And these

36

feelings went so deep he could guide them even by starlight.

Here in the flood-plains the foliage grew super-fast feasting on the rich silt spread out by the flooding river. The quick growth meant that Nawo's team had to cut a fresh path every year. Nothing ever remained in the flood plains one year on to guide them. It was hard work cutting swathes through the bushes and chopping a path through stands of fast growing immature trees. Teams of the strongest men came forward so that there were always fresh bodies doing the work and it seemed no time at all before the work was done. It was almost a competition to see which team could cut the most and the work just slipped by so fast.

Nawo knew where to look across the plain and empty pages of these flood plains and river valleys to find the 'writing' on the sides of the hills. The hills that had once been carved out into ancient roadways by the early humans. Everyone followed and the passage of so many feet made the long vanished and hidden paths on the hillsides become real until they overgrew again before the next time the journey came around.

To avoid the waste lands they had to go over the coastal mountains to the rain shadow plains inland before heading south again to where they would cross the big river. This was a river that was too wide to cross nearer the sea so there wouldn't have been any point in going through the half life lands anyway, they would still have to go inland at some point.

It had rained steadily all night, at times so hard the noise woke them up. Nawo had checked around the shelter several times in the night to make sure the run-off was not coming in. By the time everyone was awake the rain was trailing off and had ended when they started walking. It was typical of the coastal regions at this time of year. Looking down towards the sea the clouds turned from almost uniform dull grey to a strip of brilliant blue-green that had a trickle of coal grey clouds hurrying across it from the tops of some of the hills. Below the blue-green strip was another layer of clouds, brilliant white at the upper most tip from an unseen sun all the way down to dark grey where it met with the earth at the horizon. It looked like you would have to be able to fly before you would see the sun this morning, at any rate. It was much warmer today and the cold that had promised snow several weeks ago was long gone. That was good. Snow was not something they could handle in much more than a light dusting. It was the main reason they stayed as near to the coast as possible. Here in autumn, when it did snow it didn't last for long. Inland after the first snow it stayed like an ice age through winter and into spring. At the coast that yearly return to the ice age didn't start until winter and they would be long gone from these parts by then.

As the children grew they looked at the trees in the forest and the plants in the glades, and wondered at the beauty of it all, it was so new to them. The journey became the most important part of their lives. Every year they identified themselves with every part of what they grew up with, and every part which grew up with them as well. Places had names that remembered things that happened sometimes many lifetimes ago, like Callie's Creek, because Callie had fallen in while crossing it on a log but so slowly and with such arm waving and commotion that everyone had time to turn and watch. Afterwards she and everyone had laughed so loud while she dried in front of a fire.

Even the giant firs had names. These were the ones with trunks wider than five men could stretch their arms at the base. They were seedlings back to the days of the early humans. The children named everything that impressed them and the oldest trees of all had many names. These mighty beasts gave a dignity and silence to the deep forest that was almost mystical, it was as if in their presence time was standing still. And in a sense it was, they were a snapshot of the tens of thousands of years of all their past—They represented the beginning and the end of everything that was life for us. They represented time itself.

In the clearings there were blackberry tangles covered with delicious fruit, salmon berries both creamy coloured and soft and sweet or strawberry red and tart, and there were all manner of other bushes and shrubs some with edible berries. The blackberries and salmon berries had this wonderful trait of ripening a fresh batch of berries each day, so as each day of the journey passed by there were always ripe berries for everyone all down the line. Where there were no bushes or shrubs there were giant ferns and tall grasses wafting in the breeze making the open spaces seem like magical fairy lands especially for the children who were so small the ferns towered over them like trees. The sights and sounds were so new to the children because there was no writing so everything learned was passed on from their elders or seen first hand.

The important things were almost second nature—what was good to eat, where to find it, what signs to look for, like one type of plant always grows near another plant which was good for medicine, and of course, how to hunt. That was something everybody knew. And everyone knew how to defend themselves, how to fight, and when to run.

Nearly all these things had to be learned by the sailors, youths and adults alike and this took time, but there was always some wiggle room in the walking of the journey. There were just too many variables to have every milestone set firmly in time.

Alesha was the eldest daughter of Dee-an, Nawo's best scout. She would be seven this year when they reached the wintering lands and she was ready to mate. She knew who she wanted—Narok, but with all her best efforts she had gained only a smile from him so far. So on this hunting day Alesha waited just inside the forest edge well out of sight of the camp and as Narok returned with his deer on his back she casually moved out into the middle of the game trail in his path. Surprised, Narok moved quickly to the side of the trail to avoid hitting her. But Alesha moved even faster into his path again with perfect timing and the two of them tumbled to the ground with Alesha making little squealing sounds and ending up on top of Narok preventing his escape! With her face just above his, all Narok's indifference faded away and vanished. "It's you," Alesha said. "You're the one!" Narok looked up at her sweet face through her long flowing hair. He felt the warmth from her body radiating through him, and there in her eyes saw all the world and all the universe going back to the beginning of everything, and at that same moment in these deep dark pools he saw into the future to the end of time. He lifted his arms and placed them around her body then slowly raised his head towards hers, paused slightly and kissed her full on the lips. Now their bodies slammed together as their arms locked in an embrace that neither of them could release. About the only thing in Narok's mind was: "Wow!"

The next day there was a heavy bank of fog covering the land below them in the valley. Above it there were the dark green firs on either side on the hills. Clinging to the top of the hill on the right there was a thin layer of mist moving over and through the trees and heading off to join the thick bank of clouds that hid the hills and mountains of the interior. The hill on the left of the valley was bare green forest while the fog bank over the valley bottom slowly moved and undulated as if underneath its soft white quilt there was a giant moving restlessly in the dawn and slowly waking out of sleep.

Every day was now like early Sunday morning where everyone is waking up slow, rolling over and sleeping in. The quietness was huge and every other little noise now seemed so loud. Small streams filled the air as the water rushed towards the sea or lake. The voices of the birds were swelled to make up for the lack of sound. Squirrels were louder sentries of their territories, and then the sun came up like a flash of stop-motion lightning frozen in time so the thunderclap never has a chance to reach you through the trees.

They were approaching the top of the mountain pass now and there was a three inch thick blanket of snow fresh on the ground. Strangely enough it was rather fun especially for the youngest children who had never walked in snow before. This snow was nothing to be afraid of, it would disappear a few miles down the other side of the pass. At the top of the pass there was an open glade of pristine white snow and as they entered the open space they could hear the sound of random chimes in the distance. They smiled at each other, and at the other side of the glade walked up to the short bamboo poles suspended beneath the bow of one branch of a great old tree. The poles were different lengths and rang with different notes as a striker moved in the wind and touched the poles. As they passed by, each one of them touched the poles lightly with their hand causing them to strike against each other and to ring even louder than in the light breeze. It was a lovely sound that marked the start of their journey back down to autumn on the other side.

Autumn on the other side

Chapter 4, Lost.

Shiwobi was frightened. She was wise to be frightened. She had been trailing her parents Nawo and Shinsum and her brother Narok on the way back from a hunt and had fallen so far behind there was no sight or sound of anyone. She wasn't even aware how long they had been out of sight. Normally she had no trouble keeping up but today she was carrying on her back an extra heavy portion of the deer her father had shot. The added weight meant she had to concentrate more on the mechanics of walking over the tougher parts of the trail. She had to take more care to place her feet on the rocks or tree roots so she could keep balanced and able to maintain momentum uphill or not get swept off her feet going downhill or crossing creeks. While she was looking down in front of her everyone else had gone from sight. Of course she could have been day-dreaming a bit too—there was this really cute guy in the lead group, and he seemed to be keen on her. She smiled again as she thought of him and it took her mind off the hard work she had to do now.

Slowly it got dark but she kept on walking. Like her father she had a natural ability for finding the right path. Even as it got dusk she could see the slight marks of the footprints her family had made on the game trail they were following. This was the same trail they had used when they started out early that morning, and there were parts of it she remembered. On the way out in the morning she had looked back at crucial places and partially memorized them so she would know which way to go going back if necessary. She always did this but now was the first time she had ever needed that knowledge.

It was downhill all the way now. She knew that and it was a good feeling especially with the heavy load she was carrying. She quickened her pace and was almost jogging when, like it was the most natural thing in the world, the path started to go back up the hill. As she took the first few steps upwards she stopped and looked ahead and then back down at the path.

There were no footsteps or any signs of passage in the dust ahead of her. Panic seized her and froze every muscle in her body. On the way out in the morning they had only gone uphill at this place. So going back she must only go downhill. She realised that for the very first time in her life she was lost in the forest.

Several miles away on the edge of the forest, Nawo was waiting for Shiwobi. He looked up at the night. The clouds were spread out in swirling patterns towards the west and formed a solid bank of white towards the east that ended in flat puffs of cotton-wool that got smaller and faded to a giant hole directly above him. The cloud cover was so high it was almost one dimensional and flat. To the east a bright full moon shone through the solid bank and lit all the other clouds in the sky bright white. As he looked he could see the hole in the sky was moving east and getting bigger. It almost looked dark blue but that was probably his imagination. On the edges of the hole a few out of focus stars appeared—only the very brightest stars could compete with a full moon, even one behind a bank of cloud. In as long as it took to think about it the black centre of the sky had fully uncovered the moon and his own single moon shadow was visible standing alongside the tall dark shadows of the trees. At this time of year the full moon was called the hunting moon and no movement could be seen in all the earth around him. Only the hole in the sky moved amongst the silent clouds. An owl called out far away through the silence, and alone in the forest its prey paused and listened. Tonight as on most nights, death would come on wings just as silent as always. Only this night in the black and half-white world of the dark-white bright-white hunting moon, the earth will have a silent fleeting and unseen black shadow from above. Nawo looked at the one-dimensional colourless world around him, at the motionless cold stark grey bushes and trees. But no matter where you look in the forest tonight, death will still come from behind you as a black shadow in the night.

44

Shiwobi forced the panic aside and her arms and upper body were shaking as she turned around slowly and carefully on the path. There was one set of footprints behind her. She walked slowly back up the path she had come down, her eyes locked on the footprints in front of her as if they were the only things in the whole world. And they were the only things in her world, they were her only link with the past and at that time her only chance of making it out alive. A few hundred yards later she came into a clearing and saw more than one set of footprints ahead of her heading up the hill. She had been here before, and so had her family. She rested her pack with the meat tied on it on a big old log to the side of the clearing and slipped the straps off her shoulders. Free of the weight, slowly she walked around the edge of the clearing in the increasing dark—and found an almost hidden trail off to the side with all the footprints on it heading downhill. Yes! This was the way she must go. The trail had forked in the clearing but the one they had walked up was not the major fork so she had missed it in her eagerness to get out of the forest on the way down. She shouldered the pack once again and started off down the right trail breathing easier and with the weight of the pack somehow lighter than before.

Now it was truly dark in the forest and she was stumbling along unable to see exactly what she was stepping on. Her progress was very slow and got even slower when she reached the dry creek bed that they had started out on in the early hours of the morning. Going down the rocks and tree roots in the creek made her slip and fall many times and then without knowing exactly what happened the darkness in front of her opened up into a huge black hole that sucked her in before she could even cry out. The fall seemed to last forever with no sense of movement as though she had fallen asleep and was dreaming through space and time, and as she fell she tumbled and landed on her back cushioned by the load she was carrying. As if by magic she was unhurt, so she picked herself up and stumbled on knowing that she was almost back. Finally the trees opened up into the sky, and the stars and moonlight showed the grasslands of the valley floor where they had started out.

On the edge of the trees silhouetted against the black starlight and half white half grey clouds there was a tall dark figure facing her and as she walked closer the figure's arms reached out to hold her close.

...there was a tall dark figure facing her

A great feeling welled up inside Nawo, an involuntary breath seemingly bigger than any in his life before, beginning in his stomach and rising ever faster to his lips... almost too fast for them to open to receive the air. At the same instance tears welled up from his eyes and fell over his cheeks. It was a mighty rush, almost an explosion of his whole being that released him from the stone which he had become since his daughter's loss... to bring him back to life. Shiwobi dropped her pack from her shoulders and fell into her father's arms, her breath coming in huge gulps that were almost sobs. "I waited here." Nawo said quietly. "It was the only place I could be sure you would come. If I had gone back into the forest, we might never have found each other again." He paused. "You had to find your way back on your own." They held each other close rejoicing in each others warmth, and slowly their lives and heart beats returned to normal.

They were heading up into more mountains now and had passed south of the northern half-life lands. The maple leaves were falling. First turning colour on the trees then falling light green in the centre and yellow on the edges with stalks of amber or red. Later they would be all yellow on the thinning tree and amber brown mixed with yellow on the ground. There were flame red bushes in the valleys some burning red, others deep bright orange, and a few starkly maroon and darkly beautiful amongst the yellow maple and green-black firs of the elder forest. The sunlight in the early morning picked up the yellow highlights on the distant hills. Everywhere they walked now the lighter colours made the forest brighter and the new golden carpet of leaves lent a spring to their step as they rustled softly and quickly underfoot. The colours of the trees seemed to change even as they walked by them. A few flame red bushes were now sunset orange. The blackberries were withering and hanging closer to the ground, still with some ripe berries but nothing ate them now. Today one of the bright red bushes had lost most of its leaves and on the open trail there was a half-circle of flaming red for them to walk on amidst the glittering yellow gold.

Then it began very quietly to rain. Firmly. The sort of rain that never seems to stop or hurry. No streamlets on the ground scurrying away into the undergrowth. No fuss or bother and yet the next time you look and without you noticing, everything is soaked to the core. The maple and birch trees were no refuge from the rain. They were partially into their winter hibernation with half green and half yellow leaves fallen and ready to fall with the next rustle of wind. The water dripped off everything above them and disappeared into the beds of dark green ivy under the branches beside the pathway. There was no ivy on the path, just soft earth and leaves split every now and then by tree roots.

Hours later the rain had gone and a light breeze picked up the leaves on the trees and gently waved them dry. Later still the clouds were breaking up and splashes of sunlight hit the trees but seemingly only the ones with yellow leaves leaving those still in green hidden and almost invisible in the background. As the gaps in the cloud grew and moved and the sun moved across the sky the yellow trees moved too following the sun, or so it seemed.

Now they were back on the clear paths under where the dark firs ruled and in a bank of thick cloud. Everything was dry as they climbed up towards the highest point of a ridge and then they broke through the cloud seeing the bright sun to their right. The clouds hung all around them only just below and as they walked on over the crest of the ridge and down, the soft cold whiteness swallowed them and their world shrank to almost nothing once again. Hours went by and again they climbed above the clouds this time revealing a clear blue sky. There was a hint of yellow or faintest white where the sky touched the top of the white and speckled black snow capped hills all around them. The green trees on the lower part of these hills were now a sombre shade of dark black and they knew that beneath these trees above them on the higher slopes but hidden from this distance, was a crisp white layer of snow and ice. The chill air moved slowly down from the hidden snow above them and touched them lightly on the face, and there was no sound at all except the rustling passage of their feet. It seemed as if every living thing in the world other than the plants and trees had gone, except them, and their step quickened in the cold late afternoon air. "You are late." The forest whispered. "You must hurry now or you will sleep with me, join with me and live forever in the quiet chilling cold of my embrace."

Andrew put his shoulder under the arm of his mate Elly and lifted her to her feet. They were both so weak still with the remnants of a fever. But they had to walk, the sailors and the last families in the line were leaving, they couldn't stay here until they were better. Even if they didn't get caught in the snow and ice they would be the target of every predator in the forest around them. The predators knew that the weakest and most vulnerable were always at the end of the line. They were both quite old now, 25 for Elly and 26 for Andrew. They had never had any children but even so they had had a good life helping to care for the children of their friends. They both had favourites that they mentored and regarded almost as their own. But these children were all at the front of the line now. "You could say we did too good a job of teaching them," said Andrew. Elly smiled somewhat sadly and nodded her head. "We will try to keep up," she said.

Later that day it was obvious they were just not strong enough so Andrew retrieved some of their heavier possessions that the family they were with were carrying for them and bade them farewell. "We'll carry on resting for a few days and hopefully catch you up later when you stop to hunt." As their friends disappeared quickly from sight to catch up with the end of the line Andrew began work on beefing up a shelter to make it thicker and give them more protection from the cold at night. Elly made a fire and began preparing a meal. Although they were quite high up in the hills they were near to a stream and there was plenty of game grazing only one or two valleys away. That game would return to this valley now that the line had passed by so they should have plenty of food in a few days.

The days passed really quickly for them and after a week the fever went away replaced by a hacking deep-rooted cough that kept them up at night. Elly ground up some turmeric and mixed it with some honey and lemon juice and both of them found relief from the coughing with this. Andrew shot a deer that was one of the first to return to their valley, then the two of them prepared the deer and made a large stock of jerky over the next few days, all the while recovering the strength in their legs and rebuilding their general health.

After ten days had passed they looked towards each other in the cool crisp air of an early morning. The smoke from their fire drifted up the valley following the path their friends had taken, and their eyes followed the smoke. They both smiled and looked back at each other and without a word began packing up to start walking south once again.

Though they were walking slowly they made good time because the path was still well cleared by the passage of so many feet in the main body of the journey. A week later they made it back to their friends when the end of the line had stopped to hunt and rest. It was a good feeling for them. They shared the food the others had killed and walked on with everyone else once more, well enough now to be able to keep up.

Seeing the cotton wool fog below you covering and hiding the valleys

There were times when Nawo wondered to himself how the early humans had coped with their problems back before the wars, before the half-life lands. Why did they live so close together in what was now the ruins? What did they hunt for food? It didn't make any sense at all.

Now there were simple pleasures. A good hunt, a good year for blackberries, or a good starting of the day in the early morning mist heading up a mountain pass. Breaking out into the sun on a cool crisp day in autumn—seeing the cotton wool fog below you covering and hiding the valleys, like the top of a roughly kneaded loaf of flat bread dusted with white flour waiting to be baked. Above, only the middles and the tops of the hills and mountains stood out before the seamless eggshell blue sky so clear you could see to the ends of the Earth from the tops of the mountain peaks. In the evenings on those clear days in autumn the sunsets were to die for.

Chapter 5, The Stories.

Some evenings we would sing and dance and there were special evenings when I would tell the stories. The children loved those times and over the years they learned the stories by heart. The evening would traditionally start with me asking them what they wanted to hear.

"Tell us the story about," well perhaps, "the first journey!" one of the children would say, and the others would chime in: "Yes, yes, the first journey!" Or whatever it was they wanted to hear.

"OK. Well, a long time ago, hundreds and hundreds of years ago, long before any of us were born, the early humans destroyed their civilization with a terrible war. At the same time a huge meteor hit the earth and somehow the year and all the seasons were changed, lengthened so that either ice or heat made the earth unlivable, if you stayed in one place."

The children always looked a little scared at this point.

"Four friends that had been living up in the cool mountains of the north away from all the immediate killing of the war knew somehow that they were not going to survive the winter when that first long summer came to an end. So they decided to try and get all the way south to where they thought it might be warm enough that they would be able to grow food and could live and hang out during the winter.

Along the way they fought many perils. Others joined them. People who had survived somehow, by being in the right place at the right time. And these people were strong enough and smart enough to know that they had to travel to live. Some of these friends were pretty good at finding their way, but one of the original four had the sight and he knew where to go, not exactly, but when you have the sight you come close enough. From the sun and the stars and the outline of the hills and the mountains it was his vision that took them south to what became the winter lands. Without him and without his friends we would not be here today.

It all started one evening when the four friends had been out hunting and they were sitting in front of the fire..."

This was one of the longer stories and for hours my voice danced around and through the minds and imagination of the children and their parents gathered in front of the fire. I loved this story above all others. It embodied for me everything that life meant and everything I ever wanted to do. It was a lovely tale, but like all stories eventually it had an ending...

"On their motorbikes they had reached the wintering lands at last. Their travels were over for now but overhead the Milky Way reminded them that their journey would come again as the stars travelled slowly and silently across the sky on their constant journey through the night.

Only one child was born that year but over the next several dozen years their numbers grew, at first by collecting up survivors but then with children to the point where they split up into different family units. That was the start of it all. The beginning of the master guiders and the redefinition of our lives."

After the story had ended the children's faces were aglow with firelight and their eyes were lit up with the flickering stars in the late night sky. One of the youngest children put her hand up and said: "What's a motorbike?"

It was time for bed.

It was not all clear skies, far from it. There were many days of rain.

It was raining now and across the valley the green of the hillside was partially washed out in a white rain-mist. Behind the hillside, sloping the other way, another hill rose in an even whiter shade of green, washed out this time with clouds. Behind that—nothing but cloud. As they walked on, the distant hill became more visible and the clouds began to lift from its base. Time passes slowly, in the cold and wet of a rainy day.

Nawo looked again for the hills but the clouds had come back down leaving them only the trees in their small part of their side of the valley. The rain was bitterly cold and his lower legs were soaked. This would be a good day to end sheltered and beside a warm and crackling fire.

Time passes slowly, in the cold and wet of a rainy day

Every now and then there were tall bushes reaching up into the grey rainy sky their branches laden with luscious bright red berries. Some of the berries were starting to turn dull grey now and eventually as autumn progressed to winter they would fall from the bush untouched. Nothing ate the berries now. Whatever it was that ate them left for good or died out long ago. But every year come spring, the bush keeps hoping that they will return.

Dee-an's mate had just died from complications during her last birthing at the wintering lands. It was a wonder she had lasted this long, almost a whole year. She was a tough gal and she had hung on so her child was now old enough to look after herself. She was buried on a hillside overlooking the lake they were approaching. It was a nice place for her to rest

Up there in the sky some geese were honking, the sound echoing up the valley. Below them the mist rose up from the lake and headed towards them, covering a thin layer of fog that was pencilled in a single horizontal line stroke halfway up the hill on the other side of the lake. As the mist got closer it thinned

Now they could see the surface of the lake, clear and mirroring the hills and trees

and began to whitewash everything below them but still leaving the outlines visible. A few minutes later the mist had gone, swallowed up in an almost featureless bank of cloud to the right of them in the sky. Now they could see the surface of the lake, clear and mirroring the hills and trees, but the mirror was seemingly imperfect—without traces of the few layers of cloud still clinging to parts of the hills in the distance of the other side where they must go.

Flower and her friend Leila had gone down to a small stream to wash the cooking pots and dishes from the evening meal. Her brother Alesis was with them while her oldest brother Alex had stopped to talk to Anton, Leila's father.

In the long evening shadows leading up to dusk the children made a wonderful picture crouched down by the water's edge amidst all the shades of brown and amber in the closing hours of the day.

Anton was showing Alex how to tie a bowline and a water knot.

"I better get down to help the others wash up," said Alex.

"OK. Show Flower these knots. She's good with her hands."

Washing dishes at the stream

Alex put the short length of rope with the knots over his shoulder, picked up his pots and pans and headed on down to the stream. His eyes started to adjust to the decreasing light as he went down the steeper slope of the hillside near the stream; then a bird trilled a warning and an eerie feeling rippled through his body. He heard Flower scream and even while moving he froze in time. She screamed again and so did Leila. It was an awful noise to hear. Alex snapped and in slow motion to his eyes let out a primitive roar that came from a depth within him never plumbed before. A sound that filled every part of all the space around him, a sound so deep it was the very essence of his young life.

He rushed forward letting go his pans and drawing his sword as he plunged down through the trees dropping as fast as if he were in free-fall off the edge of a cliff. As he burst onto the water's edge there were the girls and Alesis confronted by two grippers. Alesis had his sword drawn facing the nearest gripper while the two girls had their daggers out in front of them as they stood together side by side facing the other gripper. Alex never stopped running and plunged straight at the second animal which turned to face him, its lips drawn back into a snarl that showed the front cutting teeth of a beast that was just as adapted to eating flesh as eating vegetation. Alex swung his sword and the gripper dodged and lunged, tearing a gash in his left forearm. The other gripper had ripped Alesis' sword arm open and he was lying down on his back holding off the gripper with his sword in his other hand.

The girls were really too young to help but were trying to distract the gripper that was attacking Alesis. They were shouting and dodging about and making fake stabbing moves so that the gripper was partially concerned with them and unable to finish off Alesis. Every time the gripper turned to lunge at him the girls redoubled their attacking moves and screamed their heads off even more.

Then there was a noise like the wind had brought a giant storm upon them as Anton, who had heard the distant sounds of the children screaming, burst on to the scene. Anton rushed straight to the gripper that was reaching down to finish off Alesis and swung his sword down and part way through the animal's neck. Still living, the gripper turned but only long enough to see the sword move up and slice down once more to finish off the cut. Anton now turned to the other gripper which was so engrossed with attacking Alex it never saw Anton coming or saw his sword arcing down, and it never felt any pain from the slice that severed its neck.

It was all over for the grippers. They lay dead, their blood mingling with that of the two boys and washing off in streaks of fading red that thinned and disappeared into the crystal cool blue and green waters of the stream. The boys' wounds were dressed and the girls finished off their chores while the grippers were butchered. Were it not for Anton all four children could well now be dead.

58

Over on the east coast of North America the two giant lizards Captain and Commander were moving west, travelling only as fast as they needed to find game to eat. At first they had gone south but they had come across a barren and seemingly impenetrable desert. There were plenty of small animals north of the desert so they zigzagged up and down the country making their progress west very slow, only a mile or two a year.

It was time to mate, Captain was making small chirping noises that mimicked the sounds their young made just after breaking out of their eggs. This triggered the mating ritual in Commander... making a nest for Captain to inspect and reject until it was exactly to her liking. Only then did she allow him to mate with her. This didn't take long, a few exhausting days and then it was all over, leaving Commander free to hunt and bring food back for Captain while she incubated the eggs.

Several months later the hatchlings began to emerge and soon the whole area was swarming with their brood. For only a few weeks Captain and Commander fed the hatchlings but this was where the responsibilities of the parents ceased and the brood was left to fend for itself. For one or two more weeks the wolves and coyotes had a feast until only a few baby lizards were left, the smart ones, hiding under rocks or in crevices too small for even a coyote to enter.

Today was a special day for the wiremen. This was the final of the annual championship dogball series. Evolved from baseball, dogball combined all the elements of sport that the wiremen liked... fighting, killing, blood and general mayhem. It was a vicious blood sport that left the competitors tingling with satisfaction after completing great deeds of heroism in the midst of bloody chaos; that, or crippled for life.

The premise was simple. The ball was thrown at the player by the pitcher who did his best to brain or otherwise hurt the player. The player did his best to catch the ball and run with both the ball and the baseball bat through all the four bases to score a 'run'. At each base was one of the opposing team, a base man with a large rottweiler on a leash. The base man had one foot tied to the base with a short rope so he was forced to have combat with the player. The player used the baseball bat to bludgeon the rottweiler and the base man so he could touch the base with his foot and proceed to the next one. The base man could let the rottweiler off the leash, but then there was precious little chance of getting it back if, instead of going for the player, it started attacking all the members of the opposing team in the dugout... where the opposing team would usually succeed in bludgeoning it to death. That would leave the base man pretty much defenceless when the next player came running up to his plate. Most base men had hidden knives for such situations but a knife was not really much good against a baseball bat. Even a bat held in only one hand.

The original idea was that the rottweilers would go for the ball and place it at the feet of the base man when he commanded the dog to sit. That still happens sometimes but it's far more common for the dogs to go for the player and attempt to rip his arm off and bring *that* back to the base man. It is a sport where injuries and death are common but the best seasoned players, even with permanent injuries, are regarded with very high esteem, and have their choice of many women eager to tend their wounds, feed them, and mate with them.

Blackheart was very pleased with the way the game had gone today. The leader of the opposing team had had his ears ripped off and eaten as well as several fingers of his ball hand... which meant he would not be challenging Blackheart for the leadership of the wiremen as he could no longer wield a two handed axe or sword. A two handed axe or sword was vital if you wanted to challenge Blackheart because his weapon was a two handed battle axe. Sitting at his side at the game his mate Annie the Terrible recognized he was secure again this year and made love with him that evening in a very tender mood without most of the screaming and clawing and vicious language that usually went on between them when they had sex.

These were good days for the wiremen, there was plenty of

60

food, the weather was good and soon they would have the journey people to battle with and plunder. Life didn't get much better.

Chapter 6, The Big River.

The journey people moved on and out of the smaller and northernmost of the two mountain passes to the interior. This was to stay away from the radiation of the northern half-life lands near the coast. Several weeks later they had passed the rain-shadow plains inland and got to where the big river was easiest to cross. These plains had plenty of fruit growing wild in large areas so they were well stocked with food. At the coast the river was too wide but here although much narrower the water still moved slow enough to allow them to get to the other side in safety.

Even though it was cold it was still good living. That was the thing about autumn, the weather. You could live here in these parts, in the autumn. In the bright daylight a big old half-moon partly hid behind a tiny wisp of cloud. The cloud hurried on by the moon. North and east was more light cloud until it became a thick dark bank underneath the late morning sun. A light dusting of snow gleamed pure white on the tops of the far off hills. The air was crisp and cold and thin layers of ice were lying in wait in the shadows to see if the sun would get around to warming them today, or if only shadows crept across their sparkling surface then the ice would know winter was finally here. But not this day. The sun was still warm. It was a good day for the journey to be heading south.

At the big river most of the rafts from the year before had been saved by being pulled up one of the banks. If some had been washed away in floods then new ones were made and raft construction would continue until there were enough to provide a steady procession on the water. One man, the rafter, would guide the raft and take it back and bring the next family across until there was another man from a later family who knew how to handle the ungainly crafts. The rafts held about six people plus the rafter. Here the wind always blew upriver and the small sails they had made for no effort, but took some skill to handle in the crossing.

The sailors of course were a big asset here, crossing even a wide river such as this on the rafts was a doddle compared to what they were used to doing on the Pacific ocean.

Crossing the big river

Having crossed the big river on the rafts, Nawo took everyone west down the southern bank along the remains of a wide track that had been made by the early humans. It was cracked and broken and almost disappeared in places, overgrown with weeds and bushes. Trees grew through it and the rain and snow and ice had caused gullies and rock slides to break it into pieces. Where it was still more or less intact it made for really easy walking, and they made good time. "They must have made these paths for people who were really bad at walking they are so flat," thought Nawo. If it wasn't for the trees growing up through them and the washouts caused by streams or rockslides they would be totally boring. At least the hunting was good, there was game grazing everywhere right alongside and even on the path they followed.

Once they were on the western edge of the mountains Nawo took them south through a partly forested area full of mounds of earth with trees growing up in them, and unnatural slabs of rock lying all over the place. This was another city of ruins from long ago spanning a huge area and many valleys. There were open fields here where root vegetables grew together with other vegetables that made excellent eating. As well there were small groves of fruit trees laden with fruit and fields of delicious blueberries while in other places blackberry tangles absolutely covered with ripe berries reached out with new green tentacles to further colonise their neighbourhood.

Unnatural slabs of rock lying all over the place.

A typical day was pretty tough. If there was food left over from the evening meal you ate that for breakfast, cold or hot depending on whether the fire was still going or could be revived. Then you walked until it was time for the evening meal. Pretty simple really. Wherever you were you reused shelters built by someone ahead of you or built your own from whatever was available. If you had food you cooked it or someone shared with you. If your family was going to need food you stopped walking for however long it took to hunt and butcher game, and then you shared what you couldn't carry. Those of your family that didn't go hunting, harvested greens or root vegetables and fruits and berries if you were lucky. Someone nearby was always carrying a lighted fire bundle and when material was available batches of these were made at a time out of dry grass and bark.

On hunting days the children too young to hunt would be schooled in self defence—swords, bows and spears, and hand to hand combat. It was more of a survival course than anything. In addition to developing skills with weapons these schools helped everyone to be alert and fit and able to tumble and recover back on their feet in emergencies. There were many ways to die on the journey, some of them so fast conscious thought was only enough to know you were dying. You had to be able to react instinctively with exactly the right move if you were going to live. There were no age barriers in the journey. You had to hunt and fight throughout all your life. When you could do neither from age or injury you stayed behind and coached the children. Beorn was always helping others with their fighting skills. He couldn't keep up on the hunt now so he was back there where everyone was resting, with the very young and the very old like him, or those who didn't need to hunt that day. He liked to help teach fighting as he had always been good at combat, which was one of the reasons he had lived so long.

Things were normally pretty relaxed when it came to teaching fighting skills, but they were getting closer to the wiremen's territory and there was beginning to be an edge to everyone's personality. Especially when it came to fighting. There was a young woman called Andresa that Beorn was attempting to help today but she was being rather difficult and just not trying to improve. She was far more interested in making sure she looked good for the boys when they returned back from the hunt. "Looking good is not a bad thing," said Beorn, "but it's far more important to be alive, and with the effort you're putting in to your fighting skills, you won't be alive for long." This went down like a loaf of bread that had failed to rise and was all soggy in the middle. Beorn was usually more diplomatic than this but his left leg had a piercing sharp pain radiating from below his knee all the way up to his hip and he was not a happy camper. Andresa scowled at him and went off to practise with her sword on her own down by a stream where, not coincidentally, she could also keep an eye on her reflection in the water.

A few days later Beorn really lost his cool. Andresa had been crossing swords with several other young women but he could see there was no urgency and no real effort to their work. "You need the killer instinct." he shouted at them, "Do you know what I mean?" Andresa was the oldest so she turned to Beorn and said: "Oh, and I suppose you do." She was well over six feet tall and easily looked down on him, but Beorn didn't have to try to be able to tower over her with the mood he was in. "Young woman, sixteen years ago I was old enough to be your mother's father and I was fit and my legs and arms were strong. Others said I was fearless but I knew better, I just had higher limits for fear that's all. I was pretty stupid at times, mostly by mistake—just going for it when there was no time to check things out. I wasn't particularly brave but somehow I always got away with it, whatever it was that I was doing. I had a killer instinct, oh yes, come back with me to twenty years before you were born and I'll show you *killer*. I had no concept of time and nothing scared me when I was in battle, least of all death. I was so good with a sword that I lived to be too old to fight. Now I am paying for all those good years." Beorn paused. "I can take you on a journey to before the time your mother was born and show you the fighting we did then when nothing mattered except our daring and our skill with a sword, and our youth." He paused again. "Now all I have is a memory." He pointed at Andresa. "You will find the killer instinct that I had, or you will die long before you get to be old enough to know and feel the pain and futility of age, like me." Andresa and the other young women just stood there, mouths slightly open. Andresa's face, her body and her unspoken words were frozen into stone. Beorn walked off to be by himself in the forest and sat down on the banks of a stream and threw rocks in the quiet parts of the water, rippling the surface, and dreamed of the days when he was young.

Nawo and his family didn't necessarily work harder than anyone else even though they reached all the obstacles first. They didn't have to work harder, they always had the toughest and strongest families up with them to do the heavy lifting, to act as scouts, and to provide them with protection. It worked very simply and quite naturally... If you were tough and strong you ended up at the front, if you got injured or tired you drifted back. The only family that always stayed up front all the time was Nawo's. He was the guide, he had the sight, he knew the way. It all had a natural rhythm to it, but no permanent structure apart from Nawo and his family in the lead. Everything else ebbed and flowed like the seasons and the tide without dissent or squabbles. There was too much at stake and the journey was too tough for things like that. Quarrels are a natural result of too little purpose and too much time on your hands. If we had sat down and thought about it, we would have realized it was the perfect way of life and pretty much the perfect society. But no one has the time to think of such things like that when life was tough. We humans didn't need to think when times were hard, we just did what was necessary. Unfortunately even with all our intelligence we were never very smart when the going was easy. When life dealt us an easy hand we took it, no questions asked, and we were always dumb enough to think that it would last for ever. The good times might last for hundreds of years but no matter how long they lasted, they always ended up being the toughest times of all.

There were such simple pleasures now. Like watching an old man slowly eating a bowl of stew, his eyes staring off into a distant world from long ago when he was young, his hands cradling the bowl to keep them warm while he chews and sips so slowly through his memories. I always thought there was something very good about scenes like that.

"What are you thinking of?" said a young girl. The old man turned his head and looked at the child then looked away again. "Good times with some girls I used to know." he smiled slightly, "the hunts we went on together." The child nodded her head and said quietly as if she already knew the answer: "Where are they now?" The old man tilted his head to one side and his voice was breaking up just a little as he said: "In my memory." In his eyes he saw one young woman standing in front of him, her bow over her shoulder her hands on her hips laughing. Her body strong and slim and her eyes flashing with sunlight and life. The young girl touched his arm softly, smiled and went back to her young friends.

Annette and Pete's youngest son Dave had gone out with three of his friends to hunt. On the way back with their kill distributed among them Dave was walking last when he slipped. As he went down the weight on his back skewed his fall and his head hit a boulder. There was instant blackness. He never even had a chance to call out, it happened so fast. Some time later Dave's friends realized he wasn't with them. They looked and called out and waited for him, even going back a short way until finally there was no more time. Now it was getting late in the afternoon so they just had to quit and go on back, following the game trail to where they had left their families that morning. Together their families waited all the next day for Dave while the three friends took Pete back to where they had lost Dave, and further, but there was no sign of him anywhere on the trail. When Pete and the children got back Pete walked slowly up to Annette and held her close while everyone else looked on. When they let go of each other it was the signal to everyone that it was time to move on.

Dave woke up after dusk shivering with the cold and alone. The blood on his head had dried and clotted with his hair. He felt bad and he looked far worse than he felt. Then he realized his left leg was completely numb. He had lain with it twisted under him for so long it felt like it was dead. He looked around but there was nothing moving. The whole forest seemed to have gone to sleep this night. He decided to just lie there and massage his leg. Well he couldn't walk and even if he could he wasn't going anywhere in the dark. That would be really stupid. It wasn't a very pleasant night for him. His leg came back to life eventually but it still felt very fragile. He must have stretched his ligaments or sprained his knee when he fell.

Even without any sleep he felt a bit rested when daylight came. That next day he decided to cut across to shorten the trip back by following the large stream downhill in the valley he was in. This would cut several hours off his journey back to the main trail where all the families were. He knew this was a risk but his leg was giving him a lot of pain and he was forced to walk slowly and carefully so taking the easiest route made sense, or so he thought. It didn't last. What was an easy shortcut to begin with started taking him away from where he wanted to go. But he had a pretty stubborn streak in him so he kept on walking down. Then, many hours later, everything went to hell as the valley effectively ended where it entered an impassible gorge. There were huge steep sides of sheer rock with tumbling water down below. Absolutely no way through for him. Facing the impassible gorge Dave was truly at a low ebb. Now he had to walk all the way back up the valley. Definitely not happy. Slowly he dragged himself up what had been a fairly easy game trail down but with his bad leg it was such hard work going up. Darkness closed in and still he wasn't even back to where he had started that morning. He got a small fire going and cooked some of the meat he was carrying. It was another cold and uncomfortable night for him.

The next morning he started early but his leg felt worse so he was really slow. Mid-morning he had stopped to rest his leg when he noticed a very small spider heading towards the web of a much bigger spider just in front of where he was sitting. Intrigued, he continued to watch, wondering what on earth the small spider thought it was doing heading for certain death. The difference in size was about ten to one. The small spider paused at the end of one of the main anchor points of the web and began tugging on it. Instantly the big spider came to life and darted a few inches towards the smaller one. The small spider stopped tugging on the web and the big spider stopped also. After a pause the game was repeated several times with the big spider moving less and less each time until it no longer moved

70

when the small spider jiggled the web. Now the small spider started to crawl slowly across the web towards the big spider. "You're dead buddy!" thought Dave. But the small spider got all the way until it could reach out... and stroke one of the huge forelegs of the other spider. This spider that was ten times bigger and staring staring right down at him. "That was it— *him*," thought Dave. "It's a mating game!" This was spider courtship! Now the small male stroked the female's leg up and down again and again while his back legs formed a bundle of sperm together behind him. The back legs transferred the bundle to his front legs and he offered it to the female. She accepted the bundle from him and the male backed away to the edge of the web and disappeared. "Wow," thought Dave, "that little guy just did the bravest thing, and got away with his life. Talk about dangerous love! Hang in there buddy." It had taken nearly an hour for the whole courtship and mating ritual to play out. "What a privilege to see it," thought Dave.

He got up with a smile on his face and carried on walking but it was still painfully slow going. Just when he was beginning to think he would never make it he saw four young bucks, not gripper thank goodness, appear in front of him and look back as if to say: "Follow us." Although they weren't gripper they seemed to his eyes to be unlike other deer. Was their coat a little lighter or was it the morning sun causing a sort of halo effect? Dave had the strangest feeling come over him as if they were his friends ahead of him in another life. As they walked slowly away he turned and followed them without questioning himself in his mind. Somehow he knew it was the right thing to do. They led him out up the side of the valley then over four ridges and across three more valleys. Fortunately they were travelling really slow, slow enough for him to keep up. Every now and then one of them would look back at him as if to make sure he was still with them. At the top of the fourth ridge they stopped and all of them looked back at him as he slowly got closer. Then before he could reach them they disappeared silently off into the forest. When he reached the point where the deer had disappeared he let his breath out in a sharp sigh of relief—he could see now down below him the wide valley plain that had the main trail the journey travelled on.

There were quite a few miles left he had to go so there was no way he could make it before dark. He bedded down that night without eating but his leg was less painful and his mind more at ease so he slept much better. In the morning he set off with new hope and reached the journey trail in early afternoon exhausted, tired, and hungry... but it was too late, the last families of the line had passed by and there was no one there to greet him. He stared at the tracks everyone had left and kneeled down to examine them closely. They were at least a day old. He started to shiver again as he looked around at the long shadows and the sun now halfway down towards the hills. A moment passed as panic built up in him, then he gathered himself together took a deep breath and began preparing a fire to cook some more of the meat he carried. Having eaten he did the only thing he could do, he started walking south following the tracks of the people ahead as fast as his injured leg would let him.

As he walked he sang a lullaby very softly that his mother used to sing to him when he was little more than a babe in arms. He didn't know it but it was based on a famous musical from long long ago.

"Autumns come and the snow is a creeping
down the hills to the valleys below.
Autumns come and the cold winds are blowing
down the hills and into our homes.

Your Daddy's strong and your Mummy loves him
he's out hunting to get us some food.
Your Daddy's strong and your Mummy loves him
so hush little baby don't you cry."

It had always seemed a little odd to him that the words didn't rhyme, but that didn't matter now, it was good to hear a voice in the forest, even if it was just his own voice.

He made a very lonely sight, one young boy limping along

on his own in the depths of one of the huge silent ancient rainforests of the Pacific northwest.

He made a very lonely sight

At the front of the line some of the plants and trees around Nawo seemed not to have come to terms with the longer seasons, or perhaps they had adapted too well—Even though it was the end of autumn there was a lone tree in a clearing covered hopefully in white blossoms like a bride standing alone outside the entrance to a church. In the stillness, as Nawo looked at the tree, a single blossom fell to the ground.

Further ahead on the trail, climbing up a ridge, he saw something move out of the corner of his eye. He turned his head and his hand reached for his knife, but it was one leaf of a dried-out fern atop a cluster of moss covered boulders, the fern still standing brown and glittering gold, fluttering in an unseen breeze. Suddenly they were enveloped in a light mist blown over the ridge. The mist hurried past them chilling their hands and faces. Sunlight made a triangle of rays through the branches of a fir and the moving fluid whiteness of the mist. Below them in the valley a stream tumbled and rushed towards a meeting with all the other streams from all the other valleys. As they walked on up the path the streaming and gambolling of the water became quieter and quieter, and gradually faded away to nothing.

It was cold when they got to the top of the ridge and the trees hid the sun. They moved on until the sun welcomed them in an open rocky clearing filled in places by green moss and lichens. There the scouts built fires and everyone warmed themselves while the women heated up some food. Below them the valleys were completely covered in fog and so they became the invisible ones, hidden from the ordinary world and high above, dusted with magic from the snow-capped mountains on the horizon, and warmed by the sun and the flames from the small fires. Invigorated by the smell of food and wood smoke, they rested, embracing the simple pleasant feeling of being alive on such a wonderful day.

Chapter 7, The Wiremen.

Varsa's boot had come apart at the uppers. She sat down on a rock and took it off, and her friends Annette and Pete stopped as well to help. Pete was good with leather and he got his needles and thread out while the women fixed a bite to snack on from the leftovers of the previous evening's meal. Annette and Pete were still grieving for their son Dave but the incidents of daily life on the journey like this were helping to ease the pain.

Varsa's two children came back from visiting with their older friends in one of the other families ahead of them. If you wanted the kids back from wherever they were, start preparing a meal. Food was a surefire magnet for hungry kids and kids were always hungry!

The women were laughing and giggling as Varsa made a show of trying to balance on one foot waving the other in the air as she helped prepare the food. They had a fire going and some other families stopped and joined in. Pretty soon it was a full on meal stop with the smell of cooking from many fires drifting through the forests and glades along with the wisps and layers of wood smoke mixed with voices and laughter. As Pete gave Varsa back her boot she handed him a really tender choice cut of the deer they had roasted the night before and a smile like only a woman can.

At times like these the journey seemed more like a holiday than survival, but that was good because there were always bad times coming. Not today or tomorrow perhaps, or any time you could say for certain. Even the drylands and the desert were, some years, all OK. But still you could not say for sure. Maybe tomorrow would bring pain and death but today was good and on the journey, where nothing was ever the same one day to the next, today was the only thing that mattered.

On the colder days especially those with light rain or drizzle there was less stopping and no hanging around visiting. Even the young bucks' thoughts were on walking and keeping warm and not on the young women placing themselves in line just where the young men would be looking. The path became slippery and treacherous at times like these. You didn't have to be told to take extra care. Everyone knew the consequences of a twisted or sprained ankle. But every one of them was tough and hardened through all their life. They had no fat or 'beer' bellies, just tough muscles on lithe sinewy bodies well adapted for walking or running. They stood tall but they were not all big people—It was the way they carried themselves that made them seem tall. Long legs were better for walking so I guess over time the average height went up. It was only natural. There were short people too, like Beorn, who were almost all great fighters, perhaps because of a need to prove themselves. They would half joke that they would real soon cut their adversaries down to their size.

On the really wet days it became hard to imagine what walking in the sun was like. Our memory is so short for stuff like this. Perhaps that is why we are so attracted to frivolous things like the glittering reflections of the play of sunlight on the ripples of a stream. We notice movement and we respond so well to change it is good that our world now is different every day. Change is so significant to us that the definition of success is really our ability to adapt. On the journey our whole life changes every day. For us now, nothing is frivolous anymore. Their are no party gifts or children's toys or birthday presents. No holidays, no sick days, no nine to five, no pink slips, taxes, or speeding tickets. No health warnings, no warning signs, no signs. No fences, no safety barriers, no barriers. Just you. You are alive. Yes, you are alive.

It had been two days now that Dave had been walking on his own after his accident out hunting. Because of his injured leg he was now several days behind the last of all the journey people and probably several more behind his family. He had cleaned up most of the clotted blood in his hair, leaving only enough to protect the wound on his head while it healed. He was real glad he had had the portion of deer on his back for food. It had helped him make good time up to now. Yesterday he had cooked the last of it and kept what he didn't eat for today. He would have to keep a watch out now for an easy kill. It was good that he had youth's natural ability to heal and adapt quickly. He was going to need all of that. Now as he walked he could feel his leg getting better. Also helping, the trail was fully trodden in and every obstacle overcome by the hundreds of people ahead of him. This meant he had a very easy path to follow.

Dave was small for his age but at that point in life where he would shoot up in height and stature faster than you could turn your head. This was his fifth journey south and like most of the kids his age he was on the verge of becoming a man. Even this young he had enough trail craft to survive on his own and his fighting skills, though limited by his size, were enough to provide some security against small attackers. A bear or fully grown cougar would take him down easy enough though, unless he had time to use his bow. But cougars were smart, they specialised in ambush and that didn't give you any time at all to use a weapon such as a bow.

The memory of his previous journeys south really helped— everywhere was somewhere he had been before, so although not fully remembered it was not fully unknown either. He would get to look ahead into the distance at the top of a hill or mountain pass and it was both comforting and daunting to see something remembered in the valleys and hills and in the distant mountains laid out ahead of him. It was so far every time he looked, but yet not so far because he'd been there before. Closer there were similar feelings because even though plants grow and change with time this was always the same time of year that the journey came by, so the plants were there always pretty much the same as the previous year. Blackberries here or ferns there at the base of that hill or salmon berries over there.

He knew there was very little undergrowth in the canopy in the rainforest and that there were tough grasses in the open or in between the rugged and weatherbeaten firs at higher altitudes where there was no canopy. So even while being alone and scared he had this memory, almost a subconsciousness, of what was right to see around him. He knew pretty much what he should see, and that helped to keep his confidence up.

At one place in the bottom of a valley in a clearing there was a rock step covered in blackberries, and then a sign. He could just make out the words "BEWARE OF". He looked around... beware of what? There was just the one rotting post with the almost completely faded sign nailed to it. He walked past the sign and the blackberry tangle over to the other side of the clearing. There was one more of the small rock steps, again leading no-where. He sat down on the step and looked around wondering what this place had meant to the early humans. This would be a nice place to stay if there was any water nearby. That thought jogged his memory so he stood up and carried on walking. He had to find water soon.

Finding his way now meant his life, and while one part of a forest can seem identical to another the subtle differences became like signposts. "Yes I've been this way before, this is the way." Of course, the two day old tracks from the hundreds of people he was following were like glowing neon paint—even the bare rock had a slight sheen where the path travelled on it. Shelters were always there when he needed them and there were absolutely no distractions. No old people or young adults wanting things done, no other children to compete with or lessons to learn. No need to walk at someone else's pace or having to do what the adults thought was best, or eat when they eat. All he had to do was walk as fast as he could, all day and as far into the night as possible and eat when he had made a kill.

It was close to a perfect scenario for getting the job done—except for one tiny thing... He was a small child alone in the big forest and he was just about every predator's idea of the perfect meal. Fortunately for him the predators were only looking out for the main body of people on the journey. By the time he came along they had gone back to looking for their normal prey and his path lay open in front of him through the beams of golden sunlight shafting through the autumn trees. Still, even with all this going for him Dave was dipping heavily into his lifetime store of luck. One time he came across a mother black bear and her two cubs ahead of him crossing his trail. Dave stopped and looked at them and they did the same, the two cubs standing slightly behind their mum. They just stared at each other but Dave felt no fear even though she was huge and her shiny black coat was in perfect condition. After a few moments the mother bear decided he was no threat and turned and led her cubs off into the forest.

Above the tree tops the forest stretched all the way to the distant mountains capped with snow. If you could do a crane shot down through the tops of the trees into the forest glade you would hear a faint noise as you went below the canopy that didn't belong in the forest. The weirdest sound as though it was still up high and far away, but getting closer. As it gets louder you can hear that it is a voice singing. But the voice isn't alone in this part of the forest.

"Bye bye baby Bunting.

Daddies gone a hunting."

As your eyes reach just above ground level there, a few feet in front of you, is Sheena. Her sleek amber coat is ripped with muscles. Motionless she seems to blend in perfectly with the amber and gold colours of fall in the forest floor. She is hungry but she has finally come across some deer and has been patiently stalking them, one half step after another.

"Gone to catch a rabbit skin to put poor baby Bunting in."

Then a pause.

"Bye baby Bun-ting."

The big cat's head moves ever so slightly as she hears the singing and she orients her ears and pinpoints the source of the sound... a small human. Ahh. The human comes into view through the forest on the other side of the glade.

Sheena draws herself back into the ground cover and crouches down. Deer and a small human... Oh yeah baby, such riches!

As the human comes closer he sees the deer and stops and loads an arrow to his bow. Sheena wasn't sure what was going on with him but she was hungry and knew she was going to eat one way or another. She moved carefully on her silent padded feet through the cover of the bushes getting closer and closer to her prey.

Dave was thinking: "Oh yeah baby!" as he slowly approached the deer which now seemed to be concerned with something they had seen on the other side of the glade so he was able to get real close before loosing his arrow and nailed one. As he did this the other deer panicked and dashed in every direction away from him... allowing Sheena to bound and pounce. She held her prey on the ground using a choke hold on its neck until it went limp.

Dave never saw the big cougar quietly dragging away her kill. He was far too busy butchering his deer and thinking about which portions he would eat for his meal that night.

Late one afternoon a few days later he stopped walking and had one of those ice-cold chilling feelings ripple through his body. He had crested a grassy rounded open hill and had realized... he was lost. "How could this have happened?" he thought to himself. "Everything was going fine." He looked all around him and there were no paths between the open rocks on the top of the hill. He looked back down the way he had come. There was no path there either. He must have been dreaming while he walked. He froze and then shook himself but he didn't wake up. Everything was the same. It wasn't a dream, he was still there and lost. And then like the rustling of the tops of the trees as a gust of wind approaches; almost at the very limits of hearing he realized there was a sound that was just like a dream. And like a dream where you don't know if you are awake or newly dead the sound faded away in and out of hearing it was so far away. Slowly he walked up over the hill towards where he thought the sound was coming from, and slowly the sound got louder, and louder until: "Wind chimes!" He shouted out loud, and ran as fast as he could to them. There beside the chimes was the path... he was back on the track once more!

As the days went by the feeling of dread at being alone in the wilderness began to wear off. The complete lack of human sound became like a song. "It's the music of the wild," he said quietly out loud to himself. As he walked he listened to this music and it was like he had arrived on a different planet. One where the plants and trees were his friends and the animals all looked on him as an equal. He stood taller now and when he looked around at the trees and rocks it was all his friends that he saw, smiling back at him. It was so good to be at home. When he slept now he heard the sounds of the forest or the grassy plains, but nothing worried him, nothing went bump in the night anymore. He was the forest now, he was the day and when he stopped to sleep he was the night.

Today there was a real problem for Dave, he was up high in the mountains and it was starting to snow. The problem with being left behind was winter. Dave knew that, everyone knew that. The thing about the journey was you couldn't leave too early to go south—you could get caught up in a late summer heat wave and you sure as hell couldn't leave too late. He was right there on the cusp of too late. He knew an early snowfall would probably melt and he would be able to carry on, but no one makes plans to 'probably' carry on living. One year in ten or twenty the first snow of winter never goes away.

He was walking quickly now, he knew he couldn't get out of the mountains for several days but perhaps he could get out of the high ground and into a valley, he could find a place to hole up there. Maybe there wouldn't be any snow lower down. The path started to go downhill but now the snow was falling heavily, it was like a blanket had fallen over his world. The normal forest sounds had disappeared and he could only see fifteen or twenty feet in front. The snow on the ground was thick enough now to slow him down but he wasn't giving up without a fight so he kept walking as fast as he could. Finally the snow was so thick his feet became heavy as the snow packed up on them. His steps became shorter and on uphill stretches each step slipped backwards about the same amount as he moved forwards.

Finally as he was approaching his limit of endurance he came across a lean-to made by the people ahead of him and he gratefully set himself up inside. He went back out to gather a bunch of firewood—enough to last him through the night.

Sitting in front of the fire he warmed his hands and watched as the steam rose off his clothes and some game meat cooked. He was OK for food for several days if he was careful.

There was nothing left to do now but wait out the storm.

On the morning of the third day there was a clear sky above. In the distance it was powder blue changing to a pale powdery orange just above the horizon. On the horizon was a retreating layer of coal-grey cloud disappearing as though someone had cast a fine weather spell above his lean-to. Directly above him were a few small flecks of cloud turning bright orange from the dawning sun. Behind these flecks of cloud was a crystal clear bright blue sky. On the other side of the valley the snow-covered trees were turning into brilliant yellowy white fire as the sun hit them.

Dave explored the trail he was following but it had almost disappeared in places covered in a foot of snow with branches drooping down to block it laden with more thick heavy snow. It would be easy to get lost in this jungle of whiteness.

He did surprise a large hare which he shot. This would keep him fed until the snow melted enough that he could carry on.

Back with the main body of walkers many days ahead of Dave, the line slowly wound through the plains and into the tall hills to the south. As they travelled south, autumn travelled with them—rather as though they were stationary in a time machine. Walking was a good pace to keep in step with the change in the season travelling south across the globe towards the equator. The effect for the journey people was like they were surfing a series of waves heading to a distant shore. If you started with the first of the waves you still had time to slip backwards and catch another, but you had to hope there would always be another wave before the icy grip of winter broke.

For them there was no apparent change in season but if you turned your head and looked back far enough, winter was a little closer every time you looked.

It took many weeks to get to the foothills surrounding the Lonely Mountain and when they got there their path kept them to the west of it. Over the tall foothills they went and into the territory of the wiremen, near the huge pyramid of the solitary mountain covered in snow.

The wiremen were an ancient enemy of theirs, a people who lived in caves in a range of mountains just to the south. The caves had hot springs, and the wiremen survived in part by plundering the journey people to supplement their food stocks to allow them to last the winter hidden deep in their caves. It was known that the wiremen would take some of them captive, using the younger women for breeding, and while no-one knew for sure, it was rumoured that they kept other captives to be slaughtered as fresh meat in the heart of winter. The wiremen were known as a crude and beastly people and regarded as an almost sub-human species. Their language was frequently a guttural and almost unintelligible series of grunts and snarls. But then, in the middle of a life and death sword fight amid the screams and moans of the wounded and dying, perhaps we didn't sound much different either.

They were getting closer to the ambush zone and the men were becoming more watchful. The women and children too made sure their daggers and swords were ready. Coming up to the high altitudes near the mountain over the brow of a shallow hill there was a forest that had burned and died leaving broken

83

burned stumps along the way. As they passed the stumps the families used them for target practice, both men and women. Most of the women carried bows, not just those who had lost their men. They didn't know it but this year some wiremen were hidden nearby, watching and looking for the ones who were the least sure and steady, noting those that missed or fumbled or took longer to fire a second time. The wiremen knew the weakest were near the end of the line and they were always after the easiest prey. They wanted slaves and meat with as little trouble as possible.

Beorn had fallen back from his family again towards the end of the line and was with his old friends Junga and Mace and their three children Alex, Alesis, and Flower.

Flower was almost one year old and carried a small dagger. She stayed close to Mace and if they were attacked she would be the last to die. Alex and Alesis were at the end of their childhood. Alex is four and nearly old enough to be a young warrior, he is starting to learn how to use his bow and sword with skill, while Alesis is three and a stocky young lad with an impish grin, powerfully built but not a natural fighter. He is good with plants and gardens and likes to make things grow.

Neither of these boys could fight fully grown men successfully by themselves but they would help protect Mace from being outflanked. Junga and now Beorn were their main defence. These two would take many wiremen to their deaths before they too died. Old as he was, Beorn would summon the fires of his youth when the time came, and although slow he would be a fearsome adversary, fighting with no thought of death, able to fight with no risk to his life because as he said, he had already lived his life.

As they approached the usual ambush points Junga said in a low voice: "It is good to have enemies, because you know then where the danger lies."

That was one of the benefits of life now, we knew where our enemies were, and they knew where we were. It was all very

84

simple, we never had to watch out for the people travelling with us. None of us would ever dream of harming a fellow traveller. All we had to do was help each other along the path if necessary and fight together when the time came. In terms of fighting skills there was really nothing to choose between us and the wiremen, it was just the luck of the draw who came out on top in any one fight. We were the good guys and they were the bad guys so although we never counted up too closely, we figured we always won, overall.

Of course if you'd asked the wiremen, they would have answered pretty much the same. We were a bunch of nomadic bad guys passing through their territory and killing their game. They would have said that we deserved everything we got from them and that although they didn't actually count up, they knew that they came out on top every time, overall.

As they got into the high slopes close to the Lonely Mountain, Pete took Flower aside and said there was something secret he wanted to show her. "You must make sure no one ever follows you to this place. I showed my son Dave, but he's gone now and I must show you so the memory will stay alive."

They walked a winding path on several trails sometimes doubling back and all the while Pete was watching behind and all around. "You have to be extra careful here. This is the wireman's territory."

Finally he crouched down and motioned for her to do the same. He paused looking around and listening. "I found this by chance when I was young like you and I have guarded its secret ever since. There was once a colony of early humans here and they left this behind when they disappeared long ago. I keep this secret because, with care this will last us an age of lifetimes for the good of all. This place is for you and you alone to know about, and pass on when your time to leave comes." He paused looking seriously at Flower. "Guard it wisely."

Flower was wide-eyed and could only nod her head slightly she was so overcome by the drama of it all.

Then Pete reached down and started moving some rocks and gravel carefully to one side. He moved a couple of bigger rocks and finally some more smaller ones until the door of a dull silver steel cabinet appeared. He cleared out the last of the dirt from in front and opened the door. Inside was a huge quantity of small packets made out of several layers of a translucent material that appeared to be waterproof. Pete cleaned out some water that had got in and selected four of the packets and gave them to Flower. Then he took one more for himself. He looked at her as she crouched there wide-eyed holding them in her hands.

"Keep these hidden for a few days."

He reached back inside and pulled out a pair of scissors and gave it to her. He pointed at the packets.

"Needles and thread," he smiled. "For sewing, it's not just for men."

When they got back to their families the sun was starting to go below the tops of the trees and sending shafts of light through the world around them. In any other place on earth this would have been a lovely time of day.

Early that evening they could hear shouting ahead over the brow of a small rise. There in a clearing in the trees were several of the sailing families being attacked by wiremen. These families were friends of theirs. The children were crouching against a rock outcrop while the parents and a bunch of young men and women fought a group of about eighteen wiremen. Beorn, Junga and Alex fitted arrows to their bows and without a word ran silently forwards, dodging through the trees. In range they unleashed their arrows. Barely pausing to reload they released their second volley. Three wiremen lay dead and the others, surprised and some wounded, ran and disappeared half dragging and half frog-marching a small number of the male sailors they had captured.

That night they dressed their wounds and ate while always one kept guard. They talked about the wintering lands to the sailors and how good the winter fruit would be. They talked about many things, but not one word about the rest of the journey or what had happened on this day.

They had not expected the wiremen this soon and the word was passed on back down the line and forwards as well where they caught a faster group of families resting while they hunted. By the time word reached Nawo of the attack his lead group were already on full alert. They were several days ahead and walking up the remains of an old trail heading east so as to bypass the shorter route in the gorge south of the Lonely Mountain. The direct route south was the stronghold of the wiremen.

There was no passage for them south on the direct route, only death.

Chapter 8, Ambush.

The next couple of days passed with increasing tension for Junga, Mace, Beorn and the friends they had saved. They had banded together more closely with several other groups most of them sailors and were walking together and camping for the night as a unit, setting up guards whenever they stopped. They too were now heading east on the old trail and expecting trouble at any point. They didn't have long to wait.

On the morning of the third day after the failed attack they had been walking for only a few hours when it happened. They could hear the dogs before they saw anything. It was a chilling sound coming at them seemingly without any real direction through the low cloud and early morning mist. They didn't know where to look and their faces darted about left and right as the sound of the dogs of war came at them from everywhere and nowhere. Then the animals came over the brow of a hill loosely covered in trees still partly hidden in the mist. Behind the dogs were about four dozen wiremen, shouting and hollering and leaping in the air towards them as they ran. Most of the wiremen carried spears and swords but a few had bows as well and they paused when they were within range to loose off their arrows.

The wiremen were a fearsome sight. Dressed in animal skins like the journey people but with headdresses of horns and feathers that made them appear taller and more powerful. All of them had body paint with charcoal black around the eyes and flame-red ochre around the mouth as if they had just been feasting on raw bloody flesh.

The families had been ambushed where there was no cover except for the trees on the hillside that the wiremen were charging through. Some distance further ahead of them on their path was a rock outcrop that would have made a good place to stand and fight but it was too far away for them to reach.

Beorn straightened up to his full height of old. All his senses came alive into a flash point of power and strength, and the pain of his body vanished as the days of his youth came rushing back. The men and fighting women and youths formed a semicircle around the older women and the young children. They responded to the shouts of the wiremen with their own war cries and these sounds of battle echoed throughout the hills and mist and cloud all around them. One line was formed kneeling down at the front, and they loosed their first volley at the dogs. The line behind stepped forward, kneeled, and loosed off their arrows, killing all the remaining dogs bar one huge animal that came charging into their line going for the throat of a young woman. Beorn stuck the vicious beast through with his sword and ripped its body apart. They had time for only one more volley of arrows taking down about a half-dozen of their attackers before they were fighting hand to hand.

Beorn had been hit in the side of his chest with an arrow but he was fighting like a madman and making a huge impact on the wiremen. He had three of them engaged having already killed two others. It seemed as if he was invulnerable and although he was taking cuts to his body it made no difference, he just fought on and those he fought fell beneath his sword.

Alex was close to Beorn, fighting one of the smaller wiremen. Using two hands on his sword, he swung and crossed blades. Pulling back, he shouted with all his voice and swung again. The wireman fell and Alex leaped at one of the others attacking Beorn. He knew now what his mentors had said when he was learning to fight... "You can see the other person's eyes and if you cross swords enough times you get a sense of who he is and you begin to know that you're trying to kill someone who might have been your friend in other times. But you also know if you don't kill him he will kill you."

Battle was such a chaotic affair. In some ways it was just like the mock fighting and practice they did as children, with each person looking for an opening in the other's guard, dodging, weaving, feinting and then seeing an advantage and risking all by lunging out to make a cut. But now in the real deadly game, an advantage over your opponent was as much attitude as skill.

It was the way you felt about yourself and how you handled the combination of all the visual cues and their timing together with your aptitude for maximising the transient opportunities that occurred—all the while having a mind clamped shut like a vice on the one task at hand: Kill, them.

These things were so important but, always in battle, as in life, of all the things to have, the most important one of all, was luck. The battle cries had been heard from the line ahead of them out of sight and about three quarters of a mile away further up the valley. The fastest and strongest men and women from those families ahead ran back like the wind and silently together as two groups, one slightly faster than the other. They ran so fast their hair streamed out behind them almost horizontal so that they looked like birds of prey in flight diving down out of the sky.

The battle was at its peak and the families being attacked were in a desperate condition with half of them being killed. Even though the families had killed so many of the attackers, the wiremen were winning. By then every one of them was fighting, even the smallest child, because they knew now that they were going to die.

The first group of runners charged around the formation of rock into view and as they did so let out the most awesome cry, a sound that of itself seemed enough to wake the newly dead and bring them back to life. The fighters hardly paused but enough to see who it was and then continue with their combat, but now the clouds had changed, sunlight was shafting through and it was the wiremen who were fighting for their lives and their survival. By the time the second rescue group had joined the battle the wiremen were looking to escape, but only a very few made it out of sight back up through the trees into the mist and over the hill.

It was all over so soon and in that brief moment of time their lives had changed beyond all recognition. Heartrending cries and low moans of pain and anguish from the wounded and dying mixed with urgent calls for help to bandage them, or for those so badly injured they only had a few minutes or seconds left to live, for help to terminate the pain for ever.

Half of the rescue group went back to their families in case they were attacked while the others helped the wounded. There were about a dozen injured, but mostly in their upper body and arms, so they could still walk.

Junga and Mace were alive and injured, but not badly. Alesis and Flower were uninjured. Their eldest child Alex was dead, Mace found him lying beside Beorn. She kneeled down and cradled his body in her arms and rocked him gently side to side as if he were still a young baby, then she kissed him lightly on the forehead and placed him back down to rest. Beorn opened his eyes and smiled at her and she reached across his body to clasp his hand lying on top of his chest. "We're OK," said Mace. "Thank you, thank you so much." Beorn nodded his head slightly and spoke so softly Mace had to put her ear almost touching his lips to hear: "There's no pain anymore." His lips stopped moving as he slipped quietly away while tears fell down Mace's face. Beorn and Alex were lying among a group of eight or nine wiremen that they had taken with them on this, their last journey.

Among the dead of the wiremen was a lithe young warrior, tall with long flowing golden hair. She was the first woman they had ever known to fight for the wiremen. As they began moving the dead to put them near the fire they were preparing, she stirred and opened her eyes. She was not dead but wounded and had been stunned into immobility. As they bandaged her wounds she spoke to them proudly, not with the rough and coarse voice of a wireman but with the sweet tongue of one of them. As they listened they found out that she was one of the journey people who had been captured as a child many years ago. Her name was Firefly. She looked at them with big wide-open eyes. It was a look that had a hint of fear mixed with hope. Now, once more, she was back home with her people but could she live with them again?

They gave all the dead, both wiremen and their own people, the warrior's ending, by fire, sending them onward on the path of their final journey.

Mead was one of the rescuing warriors, and as he prepared to return to his parents he caught sight of a young woman he had long admired. Brianna was standing a little apart from everyone, tall and slim and alone. She was injured on her left arm and body with sword cuts, but not badly. Her parents had died alongside her in the battle. She looked proud and yet so sad, and although she was standing in the midst of so many people, it was obvious she was standing there alone.

Brianna felt Mead looking at her and slowly turned her head. Their eyes met and the sounds and visions of the world all around them disappeared out of focus and quiet below a whisper. A tunnel outside of which it seemed was swirling clouds and fog formed between them, each standing on the entrance alone with each entrance edged in sunlight. An instant passed that could have been an age, then Mead walked to join her and in the distance Brianna moved to join him. Briefly they touched both hands, arms outstretched in front of them and then embraced. As they held each other close people moved like ghosts in and out of the swirling mists surrounding them inside their eyes. The mists enclosed a globe that held only the two of them. A globe that was their whole world now.

They left together after sharing the belongings of her parents and headed off to join his family's group where he had left them up ahead.

Junga and Mace were helping redistribute the belongings of those who had died. "We'll call our next child Beorn," said Mace. Junga nodded and reached out to touch her. She moved to him and they clasped each other in the middle of all that heartache in an embrace. Their thoughts dissolved into the layers of cloud and mist still drifting about them. But these mixed now with the shadows from the morning sun slowly eclipsing the fading sunlight of all their dead friends and family that had gone. Gone forever.

The snow had melted enough for Dave to continue and although he was now even further behind the main body of walkers he could still easily see the path they left behind.

He knew he was in real danger when he reached the wiremen's territory. There was not anything he could do to stay hidden in the open plains leading to the Lonely Mountain, so he kept a constant watch for any movement all around and especially in the direction he was heading. As he got closer to the mountain he got into the forest and here he took extra care to be quiet and tried to walk around open clearings keeping to the trees and brush, only crossing places where there was no cover after waiting and watching for movement of any kind. On one of those waiting periods he was just about to move on when out of the trees on the other side about a hundred feet away came three wiremen. Dave froze, not even moving to crouch down, and watched as the three men walked casually across the clearing and out of sight following the trail made by the journey people. "Oh shit," thought Dave, "they're going the same way. I'll never get past them." He stayed still trying to make up his mind what to do and then out of nowhere there was a rush of air and 'thunk' as an arrow slammed into the tree next to him. At the same time Dave saw one of the wiremen rushing at him out of the trees to his left wielding a sword. Like lightning Dave notched an arrow, pulled back on the string and launched it into the heart of the wireman at point blank range. He fell motionless at Dave's feet.

Desperately, Dave looked around but could see nothing of the other two. "I'd better move," he thought, "they know where I am." So he ran quickly off round the clearing in the direction the wiremen had come from and headed off the trail into the thicker brush and crouched down, keeping his eyes looking all around him. For a while nothing happened then there was a slight rustle of bushes and the two remaining wiremen walked past him about twenty feet away. Without thinking Dave pulled back and nailed the second man, dropping him to the ground, dead. The one in front swung round and launched an arrow at Dave but missed as Dave dodged to his right. Dave had an arrow notched and as the wireman loaded his next arrow Dave fired and killed him.

Quickly Dave retrieved his arrows from the bodies and carried on following the path of his people. Now he was in fight and flight mode and he didn't try to walk quietly or stop and look when he got to clearings, he kept moving quickly. He just wanted to get the hell out of this part of the world.

He could see where the fighting had taken place and passed by with great sorrow where the fire had been burning the remains of the dead from the big battle.

His leg was almost back to normal so he made good time on the gentle slopes and level plateaus to the south east of the Lonely Mountain. Here he was well clear of the wiremen and his heart was feeling a bit lighter so he let his pace slow down to normal again.

There was a pack of wolves ahead of him that were tracking the last people in the line. "There must be some other game they are after," he thought. "Wolves never attack us."

He was much closer to the end of the line now because the attacks by the wiremen had caused a day to slip by and then everyone slowed down to allow the injured to keep up. Judging from the footprints he figured he was less than a day behind, perhaps he really would make it back after all.

Chapter 9, The Pass.

Junga and Mace's party walked only a short distance on the following day because some of the injured were very slow on their feet and all the while Firefly was noticeably upset, looking about her and pausing as if unsure of what to do. She was acting perhaps as if she had a fever. In the early evening as they prepared food over the campfires she was standing alone facing back the way they had come as if waiting for something. Junga moved to her side and followed her eyes into a distant grove of trees standing on a small knoll. Seconds passed like minutes and then there were three people standing in front of the trees. A man, a woman, and a small child.

Seconds or perhaps minutes later Firefly moved towards them and in the distance the woman let go the hand of the young child. Firefly and the child walked towards each other, faster as they got closer until they were both running. Just before they met she kneeled down to scoop the child up and hold him closely in her arms taking most of the weight in her one good arm as she stood up.

Junga had not moved and there he waited.

This way they stayed until at last Firefly looked up at the couple by the trees, nodded her head and put the child down. She paused, looking at the couple, then raised her hand to them in parting, and together with the child, turned and walked back to Junga.

"My son Rohan. His father is dead in the fighting these last few days."

Junga looked up and back at the distant trees and there was no-one there.

It took them over a week to recover from the attack by the wiremen. They still had to move slowly so the injured could keep up, and all the while they were falling behind the main body of families. As they climbed over the hills inland through the mountains and into the plains, Junga and Mace and their group became the last people in the line.

Firefly was walking with Junga and Mace. She and Rohan had become part of their family group. It was a common enough situation when one partner died. Junga had strength to spare and Mace a sweet disposition towards Firefly. Rohan was busy learning all the ways of the journey that were so new to him from the other children. All the while Firefly knew Junga was well attracted to her and that Mace did not disapprove. It was a good and pleasant way for everyone to live.

After several days on the plain it was time to head back over the mountains towards the coast. They had passed the stronghold of the wiremen and needed to be closer to the sea in case of an early winter storm.

At the almost disappeared and hidden remains of a big city Nawo led them out of the plains and into the hills where there was a gorge that would lead them up into a mountain pass. Only a short way into the gorge there was a place where a huge rockslide had fallen. An entire hill had collapsed, wiping out the pass and leaving a sheer loose face about half a mile wide that was impossible to traverse. The other side of the river was also sheer and impassible and the river way too deep and fast for them to cross anyway.

Nawo looked at the hills to the north. In his mind he was plotting a route for them to travel. He knew it would not be easy but there was no alternative. He led everyone back a short way until they could walk north up a small valley with a fairly big creek. A mile later he found a game trail on the steep slopes of the western side of the valley on the other side the creek. Nawo stopped everyone and he and Dee-an went ahead up the trail to check it out while all of the other scouts went to see what there was further up in the valley.

The small trail zigzagged up through the trees and it took nearly an hour and some scrambling on the loose steep bits before the two of them got to the brow of the hill. The trees had thinned out as they got closer to the top and they could see across the next valley to a much higher hill to the west. "It may be tough to cross that valley," said Nawo. "But there's a plateau on the top of that hill over there and I think it will lead us back into the gorge on the other side. We may have to cross several more hills, but eventually we'll be OK and well get back to the gorge."

"I don't think we have a choice."

"Right. We'll find out when we get back down and hear from the other scouts, but even if there is another way higher up by the creek this is probably more direct. I seem to remember that there were old pathways that went up into the hills ahead of us here, back when we were able to walk through the gorge. We'll find one of those and it will take us back to our normal path in the gorge."

When they had almost got down the hill all they could see as the people came in to view were faces looking up at them through the trees. Some hopeful, some scared, most of them somewhere in-between, but all of them looking up at Nawo. The scouts were back and the decision was easy—there was no way to get out of the valley further up as it just got steeper and rougher until it became a mess of huge fallen trees covered in wet moss, tumbled boulders and steep impassable cliffs with water cascading down them.

They restocked their water supplies in the creek and everyone started the long hard climb up the hill. As Nawo had thought the next valley was tough to get across with boulders and rocks piled over each other in such a way there was no possibility of a path, each of the bigger boulders had to be climbed over and the younger children carried by relays of the adults. As well, hampering everything, there was thick undergrowth that had to be cut down. As they made their way through the valley everyone in the line moved rocks and logs to fill in holes and generally make something of a path to walk on, so the way got easier for the people towards the end of the line. But when they finally made it out up the other side, the plateau was almost bare of trees and easy going and they made good time once again. There was a lovely view of distant mountains from the plateau but no-one was interested in looking, least of all Nawo. He was focussed ahead towards the end of the plateau. If you had known him well you would have seen in his face a tension bordering almost on doubt and desperation. But Nawo was leading, he was the one in front so no-one could see his face.

After what seemed like hours they were almost on the other edge of the plateau when Nawo saw it—the faint traces of a wide path off over to their right in the distance. His pace quickened as he led everyone towards it. Once he got to the start of where it had been, the path seemed to have disappeared almost entirely so he moved his head slightly left and right and changed his direction as he walked so that the faint signs made sense to him—rocks slightly in line with others further ahead, a general absence of rocks where the path should be. Not much to go on, but enough for Nawo. A half-mile later as they got to the steeper slopes leading into the valley the path was easily visible to everyone and carved deep into the side of the slope. Nawo looked back and Dee-an was smiling at him. He smiled back, nodded his head slightly and his face and body relaxed. He knew where he was going now!

About five miles later they were back on the very wide path in the gorge and everyone all down the line was smiling and talking and walking at their normal pace once again.

Junga and Mace's friend Anton was one of the older men from the rescue party that had saved them in the attack. He had been badly injured by the wiremen. He had lost a lot of blood and had been struggling for days to keep up with Junga and Mace's group. Now he could hardly walk. He was limping and barely able to lift his feet as they climbed steadily upwards in the foothills. He sat down and rested often. Finally this was it for him, the end of the road, he was not able to move anymore. Junga and Mace and their children Flower and Alesis hugged Anton goodbye. All the other families in this last group touched him briefly on the knee or shoulder and left him alone sitting down on a rock in a clearing on the side of the trail. Flower had given him a short length of rope before she left and holding it on his knees she had tied the two ends into a water knot. Anton touched her on her hand and smiled at her but Flower was crying when she left. After everyone had gone Anton could barely see through the darkening mist in his eyes. But he could see well enough in the trees across the clearing several grippers that had been shadowing them all day, staying more or less out of sight. Now the animals stopped and waited, looking through the trees at Anton.

As the hours went by his breath became short and rasping and the sound of the forest disappeared, replaced by a ringing in his ears. His vision faded more and everything around him started to blur and mix together. But while this was going on his mind was travelling clearly through all the good paths of his youth and he was seeing all his old friends and lovers alive even though they were long dead, smiling and reaching out to him one more time, because they all knew this was for the last time. Then he realized that all the pain had gone. He smiled to himself and breathed deeply. No pain, at last. In front of him he could just make out the grippers moving closer. He held his spear up against his knee and the animals paused about 20 yards away. There was no rush, the grippers knew they only had to wait a few hours for the night.

Dave knew he was getting close to the last people in the line, he could tell from the footsteps on the path that he was only a few hours behind. But he could also see something really troubling, the tracks of four grippers following the people up ahead of him. How was he going to get past them? Maybe he could shout for help?

It was coming up to dusk when he heard the grippers snorting and fighting each other for portions of a carcass. He walked carefully forward on the trail and saw them going at it in a feeding frenzy to the right of a clearing by some rocks. He

101

moved quietly back and away to the left bypassing the clearing until he was back on the trail and out of earshot.

"Whew!" he said to himself. "That was a stroke of luck. I wonder what kill they were on?"

Now he put all his effort in to try to catch the last people in the line but it was beginning to get really dark.

Junga and Mace and their group were cooking their evening meal when Dave appeared. When Dave saw the fires and the families he was so overcome by emotion his throat choked and tears streamed down from his eyes. With amazement everyone watched this young lad staggering towards them as though he was blinded by the firelight. They rushed to his aid only to be rebuffed as the young lad appeared to be unable to talk. Finally Dave spoke. "I'm fine, I'm OK," he said wiping the tears away and fiercely standing at his full height. He was not going to be helped the last few feet—he had made it too far all on his own for that!

There was a party atmosphere that evening around the fire as Dave rested and ate and told them his story.

"You're a guide now after making that journey on your own," said Junga.

"We're so glad you're with us," added Mace. "You're safe now!"

Dave was sitting up proudly and taking his place, not with the children his size, but the other adults of the group.

The next day they took the bypass of the rockslide, crossed the plateau and made their way back to the gorge. A day later they had reached a small lake at about 4000ft. They weren't far behind the main body of people now. Eight or ten hours perhaps.

In the early evening the air was still and there was a continuous layer of dull grey cloud overhead. It was cold and the air felt like snow. Junga was worried about snow so he made the decision to keep walking overnight to get on the other side of the 6000ft pass. If they stopped and there was a heavy snowfall they would be trapped and that would probably be the end of it. They might well not get out alive.

They could hear wolves howling. It was a friendly sound, they never had any trouble with wolves.

"It's a tradition," said Junga, "that when we make a kill in these parts we leave the carcass and entrails for the wolves."

A half-hour later as dusk approached, the first flakes of snow began drifting down around them. It all looked so beautiful and magical as the soft white flakes made the normal sounds of the forest disappear completely, like they were walking in a dream.

The snow was falling quite steadily

A short while later the snow was falling quite steadily and Junga wondered to himself if they were going to make it over the pass. They were following a narrow cutting in the hill which led up the mountain from the lakeside. The going was not steep but the altitude was high and he knew that if the snow got more than a few inches deep they would have serious problems. In one place the cutting disappeared and there was the remains of a concrete bridge made by the early humans. Just two buttresses jutting out a short way on either side. They had to follow a small trail down into and up out of a steep rocky gully. It was tough going in the snow getting up and out on the other side.

Later at the summit it was snowing quite hard but only now

getting deep enough to really slow them down. They pressed on through the small rises and dips at the top until they got to the first of the long downhill sections that would lead them off the mountain and onto the last of the inland plains. As they began the long descent they came across another of the wind chimes. Each one of them followed Junga off the path about twenty feet and, as before, each one of them touched the poles lightly with their hand causing the random melody to sound out through the thick curtain of snow. But falling snow is like a wall of thickest cotton wool through which sound dies so fast that back on the path even while the chimes were ringing there was nothing but the total quietness of the falling snow.

By now everyone was exhausted and walking without thought or word, only the few feet directly in front of each of them existed, there was nothing else in their minds, just a small dream-like half globe of light white snow falling around each person, and behind, a short trail of fading silent footsteps in the snow.

Junga was leading with Mace following and their two children behind her. Firefly and her child were next and behind them were the other dozen families, twenty five in all. No-one knew how long it took but it seemed never to stop as if they had been all their lives here and there was nothing else in their whole world. Then as they got lower and further off the mountain the snow on the ground thinned out until in one glorious moment the snow stopped falling and a few minutes later the clouds halted in a bank above them that covered only the mountains behind them. Ahead there was a clear black sky filled with twinkling stars and they could see the fires of the families way below them some ten miles further down in the valley. A short while later the snow on the ground disappeared completely and it felt like magic had given their legs new life. By the time they reached the fires everything was clear above them and the stars and the milky way were lighting up their path.

It was a grand reunion that night with stories told and retold of their hardship, helped by hot food and drink, by warmth and friendship, and finally on the verge of dawn by rest that cared not for daylight and took no heed of any other thing but silent, peaceful, sleep.

Chapter 10, The Hunt.

Today was a hunting day. Four of the scouts, Nawo and his daughter Shiwobi and son Narok were about three miles from camp as the pre-dawn sky began to lighten. The deer would be moving slowly now and feeding. Overhead there was an unbroken blanket of almost featureless grey cloud with just a few layers of white and blue visible near the horizon. There were no shadows in the forest and no splashes of sunlight to step into and have to narrow your eyes and thus perhaps be seen, yet still not see.

There was no movement in the trees and bushes and the air was absolutely still. The only sound was that of a few birds waking and testing out their rivals in the air-borne branches and leaves of their domain. The forest had seen the hunters and the prey, each still unaware of the other. Both living their best life and both of them knowing what will happen but neither of them knowing where or when.

Dee-an led, followed by the other three scouts then Nawo and his children. They were on a game trail that had deer tracks made a short while ago. With each junction or clearing Dee-an paused looking and listening to the forest. The forest that was quietly breathing, not yet awake and yet not still in sleep. Like this the hunters travelled, stepping oh so quietly, and then— there they were. Seven or eight does and a buck feeding near the far edge of a clearing.

The four scouts moved slowly backwards down the path and disappeared silently off into the deep forest on either side. Nawo looked at Shiwobi and Narok. They turned and without speaking spread out on either side of the path inside where the trees were but not far, just enough to be hidden. There they became a part of the quiet forest, silent, waiting, motionless and invisible. A half hour went by and then one of the does noticed something in the forest on the far side of the clearing and all of the deer started moving slowly across the clearing towards Nawo, but not in panic, still stopping every now and then to reach down and feed on the grass. As they approached Nawo and the children they took to the path, beautiful creatures, alert, their heads up, looking carefully around them.

Without warning there was the almost simultaneous rush and thwack of arrows hitting their targets and three of the deer dropped immediately from the three unseen arrows. The others bounded off like lightning and disappeared in an instant flurry of life on the edge of a storm. So quick, day had arrived, and daylight had come with the wind. Branches and air moved and jostled with each other. The forest was now fully awake, breathing out loud, and going about its business. Just like always.

They were now on an inland plain they called the drylands. This took several weeks to get through. There was no reliable water except in one or two places in the eastern hills so they stayed close to these hills. There was more chance of hunting there as well but they tried to avoid this and just get across the plains as quickly as possible.

At the southern end of the drylands they veered east and climbed up in the valleys through the foothills on the edge of the mountains. They were heading towards the desert to avoid the southern half-life lands. There was a powerful wind behind them that sucked the moisture out of their bodies as they walked, but there were streams in these valleys so they always had water to drink. There was game to hunt too in the woods and grasslands of the hills. But all this water and food preceded what was always the toughest part of the journey—the desert.

The desert was never good for them. There was loose sand drifting all the time in the strong winds that blew there and it made for tough walking. They did their best to stay where there were some remnants of the old tracks the early humans had made. These tracks were surprisingly well preserved except for a few places where flash floods had washed them away or where the dunes had crept over them. Crossing the desert they had to go many days with only the water they carried with them. It was a place to die if you were weak and yet it was so close to their goal.

Nawo stopped early on the final day through the hills and they set up camp beside the last stream they would see for the next five or six days. There was one place where there might be water at a spring which they would reach late the next day. But there were many years when that spring was dry. So from here they had to plan on nearly a week with only the water they had with them.

There was no game that they could catch once they got out of the hills and amongst the dried-out earth and sand, but this just meant no stopping to hunt, a bonus I suppose. Also they walked longer through the day and evening and slept shorter, and so with all this got through much faster. But always it was the water they carried and their strength that defined for the most part whether they lived or died here in the desert.

Nawo's stopping earlier in the day at the stream had the effect of bunching everyone up, but everyone already knew to close up anyway. You couldn't afford to lose sight of those in front of you here. The winds would erase the tracks of the people ahead of you seemingly in an instant and then all those behind would likely die as well as you, unless you had some magic powers of direction to guide you. The desert would be a good place to discover if you had the sight, but no-one wanted to be forced to find that out here.

It was in these wide open plains where almost all of the journey people could be seen either from the front or the back of the line, two or three people wide they were like a giant black centipede winding its way across the barren waste. The wind was in some ways good because on the days without it there was a shimmering baking heat that was far worse. No-one talked here, there was no energy to spare while they walked. Even at night when they stopped their time was spent only in eating and sleeping.

Two days into the desert Varsa's mother Helen started to

have trouble. She was having difficulty breathing and was getting dizzy spells where the horizon was tilting and yet when she concentrated and looked closely she could see it wasn't moving. It was like there were two worlds, one straight and level and one trying to break away and whirl around in circles making her feel like she was falling over. But when she tried to stop herself from falling in the direction the world was tilting, she stumbled and fell over on the other side. Sitting down the world could tumble all it wanted but there was no sitting down in this place here.

The desert

Her legs had been weak for many days now and she was having trouble focussing her eyes, so that when she fell she had great difficulty standing up again because she couldn't tell for sure which way was up. Helen knew what was happening and was not afraid. She was nearing her last resting place and it would be in the desert like her mother. A resting place was where they all knew they had to go one day. Somewhere off in the hills or out in a forest glade overlooking the mist coming off a lake, or looking at the far off mountains and the clouds ever changing in the sky. But of the resting places chosen for them the desert was the most likely place of all.

This was where her mother had left the journey late one night when everyone was asleep. Helen had woken and called out but her mother just looked back at her and smiled and kept walking straight off into the night. She had been nearly seven then and was expecting her first child. Now Helen's granddaughter was expecting her first child and Helen knew it was time to join her mother in the night.

That evening when everyone was asleep she left her pack and placed her bow and sword beside her granddaughter as she lay sleeping alongside her mate. Walking away free of the heavy pack her mind was clear and her body strong again. She looked back and her granddaughter stirred, raised her head and looked at her. Helen smiled and her granddaughter nodded her head and smiled back. Helen breathed deeply the clear fresh night air, turned her head and walked off with the cold night softly touching and caressing her face. Now her eyes saw perfectly far ahead into the clear starlit night as the first hint of dawn appeared in the distant sky.

As the days went by the desert slowly changed, bushes became more frequent and a few stubby weather-beaten trees appeared. In the dry washes now there was thick scrub and more trees these ones with green leaves. There was tough wiry grass holding together the higher layers of the dirt washed down in the gullies in the rains. But the channels still washed clear of grass were indistinct and smoothly moulded into everything else by the drifting sand and dirt swept across the land by the wind.

Ahead the land dropped away from them and a few hours later they came to a small valley slicing its way across their path. As they dropped down into the valley the magical sound of rushing water surrounded them. Yes! There was water!

Word spread back down the line into the desert like a wild animal released and bounding away from captivity... "Water, water, there is water!"

As each family spread their packs and gear on the grass and boulders alongside the stream, fires were lit and those not cooking rested or prepared layers of grass on the ground to sleep on. All the hardship and danger of the desert just melted away like young autumn ice in the first rays of the early morning sun.

The stream bed was filled with bare rocks, most steely grey

but some layered with rust brown or a mix of charcoal and orange. The water tumbled and twisted its way through and over them all. It was crystal clear, cool and in the patches of sunlight... flashing bright sparkling eyes at everyone who looked.

Tired and quietly elated, Nawo and his family received waves and smiles from everyone down the line as they passed by his fire to set up their own camp for the next few days. Dee-an and several of the other scouts got ready to go up the valley to look for game and every family short on food sent people off to hunt. Between them they would gather enough to keep everyone going for the next week or so.

Amanda was a good-looking woman who had lost her mate in the fighting with the wiremen. She had two children and needed to hunt for food.

As the scouts left, Amanda was standing by the trail and as Dee-an walked by, somehow without conscious thought he came close to her and their hands just naturally found each other. Dee-an paused. "You need to hunt," he said. It was both a question and a statement. She smiled and he smiled back. "Yes," she replied.

"I know you're good with a bow," said Dee-an. "We should hunt together." Amanda placed her head lightly on Dee-an's shoulder and sighed quietly as Dee-an let his head rest against hers and then they both headed off up the valley as close to side by side as the trail would let them.

It was here Dave finally caught up with his family to their utter amazement. When he appeared walking down alongside the stream towards them they did not recognize him he had grown so much. Not only so much taller but in stature and in the way he carried himself. He stood there before them in front of the fire with a faint smile on his face as they all struggled to know who he was. "You can't get rid of me that easily," he said.

There was an uproar of recognition and he was mobbed by

everyone within earshot—and beyond as the word spread: "Dave is alive, he's back with his family!"

There was no question now—he was not a child anymore and he was welcomed as a mature young adult taking his place among even those much older than him. He was trusted now to make his own decisions and to play his full part and guide them in every incident and every adventure that came their way.

In the evening a light breeze picked up and voices were heard singing. The voices drifted up the valley mixing with the woodsmoke and firelight like early morning mist, the sounds layered and woven through the thoughts of the families there in front of the fires staring into the flames. But there were memories also lingering and watching over their shoulders from the now dead peoples who had reached this same stream, staring with them into the flames in all the many years they walked this place so very long ago.

After everyone had rested for several days they carried on and a few days later they had passed a huge lake and reached the peninsula that was the wintering lands. As they climbed over some big hills and camped for the night, Nawo walked away carrying his pack and bow and disappeared up towards one of the peaks that had some distinctive huge rocks silhouetted at the top. He came back to camp the next morning late after sunrise. No one knew for sure why he did this, always here at this one place, and always he went alone. It was just something the master guider did at this place on the journey.

In these southern hills it was like they were walking from the start of winter straight into the start of summer with nothing in between. The blossoms were already in full bloom on the groves of cherry trees they came across and everywhere it was like spring but warmer. Nothing moved but them. The air was absolutely motionless. The sky almost clear blue but with a far off hazy whiteness layered above the horizon. They were still some days from the Pacific coast so there were yet no waves for them to hear rushing and sweeping up onto the shore. And in the still air there was silence, complete and total silence. No wind rustling the grass and shrubs or gently moving the branches of the trees. All around them, nothing but silence.

Coming home.

It was like they had been lost across the seas. Lost for a long long time and now they had reached the land.

It was like coming home at last.

In the caves of the wiremen the captured sailors were put in cages and given the bare minimum of food necessary to keep them alive. It was one of Hayou's jobs to clean the excrement off the floor of the cages, but only after the sailors had been tied up so the cleaning could take place. These sailors were a different group of people than anyone had seen before and they spoke a strange language. When they first arrived there were groups of wiremen and their women and children coming by to stare at them, like it was a zoo. Hayou stared when he cleaned up as well but while he was alone with them he asked them what language they were speaking. "It's Maori, we were originally from NZ. You don't look like these bastards here." said one of the sailors. "You look like the ones we were walking with."

"My mother and father were journey people," said Hayou, "I was born here, I think my father was killed trying to defend my mum."

The sailors told him the story of their journeys through the hundreds of years they had been crossing the Pacific ocean, and

114

Hayou told his story, short though it was. One of the sailors was very old. "My name's Wally. What's yours?"

"Hayou."

Wally looked him in the eyes.

"What are they going to do with us Hayou?"

"When the game in the forest goes away in winter, they will kill you for food."

After a shocked pause this had an electrifying effect on the sailors.

"Bugger this for a game of soldiers!" and "They're a bunch of bloody cannibals!" was the general feeling among them, followed in short order by: "What the fuck are we going to do about this?"

Hayou was looking somewhat nervously around to make sure no one was listening. "You have to keep quiet in English," he said, "your Ma-ori is OK – no one understands that. I can help, I've had enough of these bastards. They're not my people and they stole my mum. I don't belong here, I'm one of you and I'm tired of being kicked and beaten. So I'm going to make a run for it. Are you guys up for that?"

"Oh you bet kid!" said granddad Wally. "We may not look it but we're real good fighters when we have our backs up against the wall."

"We'll get you and your mum out," said one of the taller and more heavyset sailors. "Just cut us loose and give us some weapons. My great great whatever grandfather used to be a forward for the All Blacks." Hayou looked blank. "Rugby, a ball game, a tough ball game. En Zed was very good at that."

"Best in the world," added Wally. "Hey, I'm old and I can't run worth a shit, but I'm way tougher than these fat ugly bastards here."

"OK, let me figure some..." Hayou stopped talking as a wireman came by and everyone went back to being prisoners and cowering idiot picking up the muck again. But if you had looked closely you would have seen a fire in Hayou's eyes that had never been there before. And the Maori now being spoken would have scared the hell out of even a mountain lion.

Several days went by during which Hayou talked with his mum and got her on board with the scheme. "We have to have food and clothing. I can handle that," she said. "Will you look after the weapons?"

"Yeah."

"OK, I'll start making a cache of everything we need."

"I can help with getting food as well," added Hayou.

"How do we get out without being seen?"

"There's a hidden cave, it's really just a small tunnel that leads to the forest, hasn't been used in a lifetime or more, we can use that. I found it some years ago and I've been keeping it secret just in case..."

"What about the forest?"

"The cave comes out in thick bush. It's completely hidden and no one goes that way. Then we stay off the main paths, there's game trails we can follow. We'll be hidden on those."

So several more days went by and no one noticed the slow disappearance of bits of food and clothing, as well as sleeping gear and packs. Hayou left the weapons till the last moment.

When the time came for the breakout there was only one wireman left that day to oversee Hayou's cleaning out the cages. Hayou walked up behind him as he was tying up the last sailor, cupped his hand over the wireman's mouth and slit his throat. The body went limp after a brief series of twitches and dropped to the floor. Quickly all the prisoners were cut loose and Hayou led them to his cache of clothes and weapons hidden under sacks full of the dirt and muck that he had been collecting and was supposed to get rid of.

Hayou had brought a pitcher of water so they could clean up and begin to feel like men again.

"We have to pass through the main cavern." said Hayou. "There's no other way, but after that there's an unused cave, a very small one, it leads to the outside. They won't know we have gone that way... we'll be safe in that part of the forest for a short time anyway. My mother is waiting for us in the small

116

cave with the rest of our provisions."

"If we don't make it you go ahead to your mum," said Wally, "no one will pay any notice of you and you make sure to take off with her on your own... OK?"

It wasn't really a question but Hayou said OK anyway and he added: "I have a feeling you will get to me. You guys strike me as being the real deal. I'll be on the other side of the main cavern and I'll lead you to the hidden cave."

Everyone was dressed and ready so the sailors crept out to the edge of their cave and watched Hayou walk across to the other side. Hayou shuffled along avoiding the groups of wiremen with his head downcast, only this time it was so no one could see the fire in his eyes. When he was safely on the other side the sailors took a look at one another and Wally said a few words rhythmically in Maori: "Tahi, rua, toru, wha." Then they marched into the large cavern that was the main living area. It was lit only by the dull red light of many fires and the wiremen were lounging around in small groups half drunk and doing nothing except waiting for their next meal. As the sailors walked into view out into the open space they seemed taller than before but perhaps that was just a trick of the light. A few people noticed them right away but did nothing, they just sat where they were with puzzled looks. The sailors had painted whirls and scrolls on their faces using their fingers and black ash from the remains of a fire. These accentuated their eyes and mouths into grotesque gargoyle-like icons which looked pure evil in the flickering red light.

The sailors fanned out into two rows facing the main body of wiremen. They crouched down on one knee and let one arm hang limply over the floor of the cave and stared intently at their enemy. By now everyone in the cave was watching and the only sound left in the cavern was the fluttering of the flames in the fires. One man among the sailors is standing. It is Wally and with a rising crescendo he screams out a challenge in Maori that echoes and rebounds off all the walls—a war challenge. As he does this the kneeling sailors slowly rise. As Wally finishes everyone is standing and everyone roars "HI" and stamps their feet. Now they go into the haka...

"Ka mate, ka mate! ka ora, ka ora!"

It is the most famous of Maori war haka dating back to the earliest days of the early humans and is designed to scare the crap out of anyone facing up to it.

"Ka mate, ka mate! ka ora, ka ora!"

(It's death, it's death! it's life, it's life!)

No one had ever seen a haka before, neither the wiremen nor Hayou and it caught them completely by surprise, so for the few minutes it lasted everyone was spellbound by its rhythmic pounding of feet and beating of fists on the chest, all in unison with the sheer ferocity of the chanting. Tongues sticking out, whites of the eyes showing, fists and spears presented with a menace that slowly became real to the wiremen and some of them started to wake up their senses and began to look around for their weapons—the weapons Hayou had given to the sailors.

With a thunderous "HI" the haka came to an end and the sailors rushed forward, ripping into the wiremen, stabbing and spearing those that moved too slow and clearing a bloody path toward Hayou on the far side. The wiremen were in such disarray they did not see which way Hayou led the sailors and, like ants when an anteater is digging up the nest, they swarmed out into the forest going haphazardly every which way—except for the way where Hayou, his mum and the sailors were actually going.

There was a great deal of satisfaction to be had for everyone as they travelled quickly along the game trails on the side of the valley, hearing, and sometimes catching glimpses of the commotion the wiremen were making in the distance, and knowing that any noise they made would be lost in the general upheaval of sound drifting through the forest.

Wally was having trouble keeping up. "I'm no spring chicken like you guys."

"We can keep the pace down for you," said Hayou.

"She'll be right mate, I'm not giving up now."

"Yeah you miserable old bastard," said one of Wally's mates, "Rattle your flaming dags!"

It took them several days to get down the valley following a big river and then through the gorge south of the caves. They had to kill several wiremen who had figured out that this was where they would go. Most of the wiremen believed they would try to escape inland along the route the journey always took.

It was snowing in the gorge and bitterly cold but the snow stopped once they got to the plains and the temperature got warmer, although not by much.

They headed almost directly south and made good time as there were still remnants of the roads the early humans built including even some of their bridges. This made their life much easier.

"We're out guys," said Hayou, "They're not following us now."

"These plains are leading us back to the journey people," said Hayou's mum. "We're heading for the drylands but we may be too late to catch up before everyone reaches the desert."

A long tiring week later and they finally came across the trail left behind by the journey. It was several weeks old.

"We'll never catch them now," said Hayou's mum, "and we won't get through the desert on our own. You need a master guider for that place."

"You've done pretty damn good so far," said Wally. "I'll follow you into the desert."

"You don't know the desert. Sorry Wally but it's pretty much the end of the world. I can't even begin to describe how bad it is. You need something I don't have. I won't take you there. I won't take you to your death."

Wally was looking a bit brute faced. "What's a master guider?"

"Something special, someone with the sight," said Hayou's mum.

"Someone who instinctively knows the way," added Hayou.

"OK, I think I know what you mean, I can do that on the

ocean, I don't need no-one to tell me where to steer."

"It's the same on land."

"Well I'm not beaten," Wally said and thought for a moment. "We're not beaten. We get to the coast, find ourselves a boat and we goddam well sail to Baja. Right guys, how does that sound to you?"

"Yeah, that'll work for me!"

"And me!"

"Back on a boat? Count me in!"

The sailors were unanimous.

"I don't like the idea," said Hayou, "but I don't see any alternative, I sure as hell don't want to just give up and die. How far are we from the coast?"

"Not sure," said his mum. "maybe one or two days."

"Well however far," said Wally, "it's all we've got left. There's got to be something we can sail there. Or we can make something."

"There's another wide path that joins this one a short way ahead, I think it goes to the coast. We'll go that way."

The ancient wide pathway did indeed go to the coast. A day later they were on the shore of a bay and there were one or two hulks of ships rotting away half sunk in the shallow water.

"Let's carry on up the bay," said Wally, "from the look of it this used to be an ancient city. There's going to be more boats. Maybe one will be sailable."

After half a day walking inland to avoid a maze of undergrowth near the water they came across another place that had held a lot of small boats and there was one medium sized mono-hull yacht that was on a large mobile launching platform. The yacht looked to be still in good condition and even the platform was good.

"Metal hull, twin keels, low draft, wow, we're in luck, this will do us fine."

"Looks like it was a just-finished a restoration, I don't see any rust outside."

"Rust will be inside, that's where it's a problem... from

condensation and no way to evaporate. But it was never launched so maybe it's OK for rust."

"Well we only need it to do one journey. It just has to get us past where the southern wastelands are," said Hayou's mum. "We can walk to the wintering lands then on the west coast, quite likely with no problems."

They inspected the yacht inside and it looked pretty good. So they started preparing it for launching. It took several days before they got the yacht into the water and several more days making her seaworthy. They had to jury rig a sail using palm fronds and then using vines for ropes.

"Gonna be fun sailing this baby!" said Wally.

"Yeah, this'll keep us on our toes."

"Nice to get back to sea though."

The morning they set out there was a light breeze which turned out pretty good to help them adjust to sailing the yacht. They travelled past a place that must have been a bridge and then the bay opened out to show the remains of a really big suspension bridge. The centre and one tower had collapsed but the left tower was still standing.

"This place must have been one of the bigger cities of the early humans," said Hayou.

Once into the open waters they set sail south keeping fairly close to the shore. They wanted to be able to make repairs to the yacht or abandon it if something went wrong.

The sea journey was a strange experience for Hayou and his mum but after the first day they started to appreciate the unhurried way of life of a sailor.

"You're lucky we have good weather," said Wally, "it's not fun in a storm."

It took them three days to get past the southern half-life lands and to where Hayou's mum figured the winter lands were on the coast of Baja. They came in really close to shore and they studied the coastline and found a ribbon of an old pathway following the coast.

"If we land here we should be roughly a day away," said

Hayou's mum, "there's only the one pathway down the coast on either side of Baja."

"We can sail further south," said Wally.

"No, the path goes inland where our winter lands are. We need to approach from the north on land so we don't miss it. If we go too far south there will be no paths, on the coast at any rate, to follow to bring us back."

It was a lazy sunny afternoon when Hayou, his mum and the sailors walked up to the journey people working in the fields and the commotion as they arrived stopped all work everywhere until the essential details of their adventures had been told.

What a meal they all had that evening, together with the retelling of their story, filling in all the details!

The sailors performed another haka in front of the fires that night to the applause of everyone.

As the northern spring was approaching, the bi-annual end of harvest feast was conducted this time by the sailors.

"We're going to make you all a hangi," Wally said, "It's part of our culture coming from New Zealand. You are going to like this. Trust me."

They organized the digging of a bunch of holes in the ground each about five feet deep and wide and ten feet long.

There was a bunch of scepticism and sideways looks from the journey people and the comments included: "Is this for burying all the people who die from food poisoning?"

The replies were good natured enough: "No worries mate, she'll be right."

Dried hard wood including cherry and mesquite was carefully stacked in the pits on top of tinder and then large rocks were placed on top of it all. The rocks had been selected so they didn't explode when they got to the super-hot temperatures created by the slow burning wood.

It took about three hours for the stones to become white hot then the ashes and hot embers were raked and dug out of the pits.

The rocks were lightly sprayed with water to remove the last touches of ash then the meat was seared on the rocks and removed. Wet hessian (burlap) was laid down on the rocks and the meat placed back. The rest of the food was then placed on top and everything was covered by more wet hessian.

Finally the dirt was shovelled on top of everything to seal the pits off.

Three hours later the soil was dug up and the food placed on tables for the most delicious feast anyone of the journey people could ever remember.

The hangi together with the haka became part of the culture of the journey people for special occasions after that, even though the sailors had become land-lubbers and their skills sailing the Pacific had been long forgotten.

End of Part 4.

New Zealand jargon

All Blacks	New Zealand's national rugby team. Famous for being one of the best rugby teams in the world and for doing a haka before every match.
Chuffed	Pleased.
Chundering	Moving at a good speed.
Gidday	Hi.
Haka	A traditional group dance and/or war cry usually performed before battle to intimidate your opponents. It is a posture dance with vigorous movements of the arms together with wild facial expressions plus stamping of the feet. All with rhythmically shouted words. Scary up close.
Half-G	Half gallon bottle of beer. A couple of half G's ensure general admission to a party.
Hi	Exclamation. Maori for Ahh! Pronounced: He
Hooray	Bye.
Kiwi	Flightless bird shaped a bit like a large pear. Native to NZ.
Long dog	Greyhound.
Mate	Buddy, friend, acquaintance.
Paddock	Field, usually containing sheep or cows.
Possie	Position.
Rattle your dags	Get a move on. Speed up. Dags are dried clumps of crap embedded in the wool on the rear

	end of a sheep. Chase a sheep and watch them rattle!
Sheila	The wife or girlfriend.
She'll be right mate	No worries mate.
Shout	Treat. Buy the next round of beer.
Silage pit	Large pit where green crops are compacted and fermented. Used as feed for livestock. Very smelly. Not good to fall into.
Smoko	Morning or afternoon tea break. Back in the day it was mostly used to smoke a cigarette.
Strewth	Golly. Well I never!
Tahi, rua, toru, wha.	One, two, three, four.
Taranaki Gate	Gate made by cutting a wire fence at a sturdy post sunk in the ground - usually the junction of a couple of paddocks, then wiring a fence post to the cut end. The gate is closed by fitting the new fence post into a loop of #8 fencing wire at the bottom and top of where the original fence was cut.
Wag	Joker.

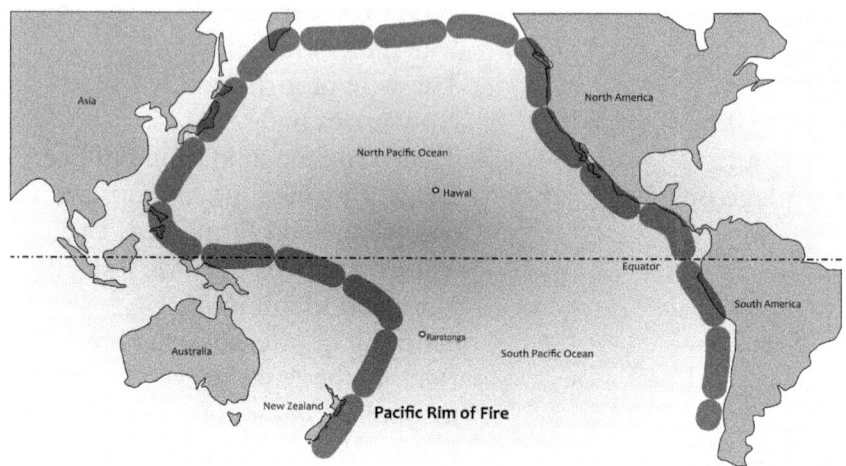

The Pacific Rim of Fire